MW00988694

# How to Silence a Rogue

The Forsaken Lords Series

Bestselling Author

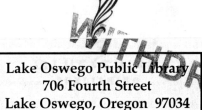

KRISTIN VAYDEN

**How to Silence a Rogue**
**By Kristin Vayden**
**Blue Tulip Publishing**
**www.bluetulippublishing.com**



HOW TO SILENCE A ROGUE

ISBN-13: 978-1543295092
ISBN-10: 1543295096
Cover Art by Jena Brignola
Formatting by Jill Sava, Love Affair With Fiction

# Dedication

*To the stud I call a husband, who inspires all the romance I write about, and to my sister. Because she's awesome.*

# Prologue

Miss Maria Garten had one more Season till she was firmly on the shelf.

One. More.

It was her only chance, because while some ladies could pretend or sincerely be at peace with the life of a spinster, she was not among their ranks.

Taking a deep breath, she reminded herself once more to think *before* she spoke. It shouldn't be difficult.

Except that it was, for her at least.

"Good evening, Miss Maria." Mr. Sheppard's voice broke through her silent scolding.

"Ah, good evening." She turned and offered a smile to her friend, the notorious Curtis Sheppard.

He bent and kissed her hand. "Lovely as always. So, tell me again why some handsome gentleman hasn't swept you off to married bliss."

"Ah, charm. You should save it for someone who will appreciate it," Maria replied with a smirk, though her heart pinched at his words.

"You wound me!" He shook his head though a grin toyed with his full lips.

Maria glanced away.

Because the only thing more certain than her potential future as a spinster was that Mr. Sheppard was a confirmed bachelor.

A rake of the first order.

Not the kind who would ruin an innocent, but the kind who would charm one, seduce her with his beguiling words, make her fall in love with the legendary smile and easy manner that seemed as easy as breathing.

And then he'd walk away to find a new distraction.

Utterly unaware that he had broken a few hearts in the process.

Maria refused to be counted among them.

She needed a husband, *not* a distraction.

After all, friendship was far less complicated.

Wasn't it?

"Have you a partner for the next dance?" he asked, all seduction and magic.

"Yes, I do believe he just volunteered." She baited and held out her hand as the first strains of a waltz began.

"Delightful! Have I mentioned how lovely you look tonight?" he asked as they walked onto the ballroom. His eyes scanned the crowd — likely looking for his next *distraction*.

Maria chuckled. "Yes, actually, you have. You must be slipping if you have already forgotten, or perhaps my beauty is so astounding this evening that you felt the need to mention it twice."

"I most certainly felt the need to mention it twice."

She fluttered her lashes. "Indeed? How kind."

"Why do I get the distinct feeling that you are insincere?" His head tipped slightly to the side as he pulled her into the frame of a waltz. His movements were light, smooth, and carefree, much like his personality.

"Because you are smarter than you look," Maria replied in a saucy manner, enjoying the freedom of speaking with a friend, not feeling the need to impress him.

"You know, that's what I've always said. A pity most don't ever realize it." He shook his head, smiling into her eyes and then glancing away, searching.

"So who is the lucky lady this week?" Maria asked, hitching a shoulder as they danced.

"I'm sure I don't know what you mean." He turned his gaze back to hers, his eyes slightly narrowing in a wry manner.

"And here I just complimented you on your intelligence."

"No, you said I was smarter than I looked. You didn't go into a description of the extent of that intelligence."

"I believe you just insulted yourself."

"Bloo— Er, drat. I do believe I did. Minx. You always were a quick wit." His lips bent upward in a grin as he turned his attention back to her. "If you must know, I'm quite taken with the late Baron Whittle's widow. She seems quite depressed. I think that perhaps I am just the gentleman to cheer her up."

"You mean seduce her."

"An innocent should never—"

"While I may be an innocent, I am not *ignorant,*" Maria replied, dryly.

"Such cheek! Very well, but you didn't ever hear me admit it."

She sighed, amused. "My lips are sealed."

"So who is your target this Season? I assume you have one. Most ladies do when the Season begins." His demeanor shifted, his eyes alight with interest.

"I'm not sure… I'm open to suggestions, if you have any," Maria replied, trying not to let the desperation leak through her tone.

"Hmm, I shall consider it. You'll need a good gentleman, an *actual* gentleman, not those foxes and wolves pretending to be charming."

"Foxes and wolves? Is that what you call yourself?" she retorted with a grin.

"Er…"

"So you think I need a true gentleman." She steered the conversation back to the type of man she needed.

"Exactly!"

"Someone with morals, with—"

"Foul! I have morals!" Curtis furrowed his brow, a frown turning his lips downward.

"They simply go into hiding at the first glimpse of opportunity," Maria replied, raising an eyebrow.

"Be that as it may…" he replied after a moment, his eyes narrowing, "…if you wish to enlist my aid given my soiled reputation and corrupt moral fiber…" He winked.

Maria resisted the urge to roll her eyes, but she smiled. "Yes, yes I'll take whatever help I can get."

So much for keeping the desperation out of her tone.

"Give me a few days, and I'll be sure to call on you, giving you a few candidates."

"I appreciate your assistance," Maria accepted with a painful humility.

"Do you appreciate it enough to end the waltz slightly early so that I may, by chance, walk by the recently widowed Patricia Whittle?" He raised his eyebrows in hope.

"It's the least I can do." Maria shook her head as she giggled.

The music was just coming to an end as they parted ways, Mr. Sheppard toward the Baron Whittle's widow and Maria standing alone.

Again.

But at least she had enlisted some help on her quest.

A friend who would come with a list of hopeful prospects.

Friends were indeed a blessing.

Friends, however, were not husbands.

And she didn't *need* a friend.

She needed a proposal.

# Chapter One

TO THE OUTSIDE, Curtis played the perfect part of the jolly and devil-may-care rogue. He was proud of that persona; it had taken hard work to perfect such a ruse… but worth it.

This was proven yet again last night when he was able to… *uncover* several leads from the late Baron Whittle's Widow. Pun intended.

Of course, those secrets were uncovered in the bedroom, but the War Office wasn't too particular how information was attained — just that it was. It was said that men loosened their tongues with brandy… the same could be said of women under the covers.

He withheld a shudder as he caught a whiff of stale brandy that the lady had sloshed onto his once-white shirt. It was an unwelcome trigger to his memory, forcing him to remember things he'd rather forget. Thankful to be home, he quickly shed the garment and rang for his valet as he entered his room. The older man had impeccable fashion sense and could tie a cravat quicker than most. Speed was highly favorable in Curtis' profession.

"Sir?" Winston raised a white eyebrow as he approached with a clean white shirt.

"You're a mind reader," Curtis replied, shrugging into the garment.

"Nothing of the sort, sir. Creature of habit mostly." He mumbled the last part.

"I'll pretend I don't understand that last sentiment." Curtis chuckled.

"You usually do, sir."

Once he was properly attired, he studied himself in the mirror. His hair was far too blond for him to be taken for a dark and dangerous rake, which is why he chose to take a more opportunistic approach to life. Having been told by many a lady his eyes were dancing with mischief, he delighted in proving them accurate in their deductions… for a time. Case in point, last night.

Yet, the whole charade had become tiresome, but that didn't change its effective nature. And when one worked for the War Office, one needed to be effective.

Always.

Straightening his posture, he strode to the door and down the corridor to find the kitchen. While passing through the main hall, his gaze settled on the one portrait he kept of his parents. It served as a much-needed reminder. Because as much as he was falling out of love with the bed-and-dash scene… it was better than falling out of love with a wife.

It was exactly what he'd seen happen to his mother. And in turn, it began an internal civil war that no one but those who lived within the walls of their home witnessed. It was horrific how two people who had at least tolerated each other to the point of an agreed marriage had come to the point where they deliberately and surgically wounded each other's dignity, pride, and emotions till nothing remained but ashes — smoldering, acidic rubble. An involuntary shudder racked his body as he tore his eyes from the cold stares and took the last flight of stairs into the kitchen.

The sounds of pots banging and cockney-accented words drew him from the tension of memory and comforted him with the familiar. The smoky scent of bacon and the yeasty aroma of bread called to him even before he pushed through the heavy wooden door.

"Ack! Sir, you gave me a fright!" Cook placed a hand to her generous bosom and balanced a tray of eggs with the other.

"My apologies." Curtis gave a jaunty bow and took the tray of eggs and set them on the counter.

"Those are none o' yer business." Cook shook a finger at him.

He grinned mischievously.

"And none o' that." She picked up a wooden spoon and shook it at him, even as her gray eyes danced with amusement. "Ye old tom cat." She shook her head.

The rest of the kitchen staff watched the interchange silently, knowing that such familiarity with the lord of the house could only be afforded by the long employed.

Or in this case, the woman who had practically raised him.

With his parents in a perpetual war, Curtis had sought out a haven from the fray and found it in the kitchen. Cook had taken him under her wing like a broody hen does an orphaned chick, and the rest was truly history.

"Ye hungry?" Cook asked, setting a plate of bacon, eggs, and toast in front of him.

Crust cut off and set aside.

He picked up a crust and dipped it in the hot tea Cook placed just to the side of the plate. "Why ask if you've already deducted that you'll feed me regardless of my appetite?"

"Bein' polite. Ye could learn a thing or two 'bout it." She shook her pump finger. "Now eat. It'll get cold if ye insist on waggin' yer tongue."

Grinning, Curtis dug into his breakfast. It had always appalled his parents that he'd prefer to take his meal in the kitchen, but they didn't push him. What he'd begun as a lad had carried into his adulthood, and he rarely ate anywhere else in this home. The kitchen was… homey. It was comforting in a world that seemed to grow more and more insecure by the day.

It was also *loud*.

Pots and pans clanging, maids scurrying about, cook shouting out orders, and cabinets opening and shutting… it was anything but what he feared most.

Being alone.

Truly, it was a defeating prospect since, whenever he imagined marriage, he thought of his parents.

And honestly, he couldn't decide which was worse: the silence in one's own home to be so loud it was maddening, or to be so betrayed by a spouse that a man would rather drink himself to death than actually live. It was the reason he played the role at parties, why he had cheerfully taken the dangerous vocation, and why he ate with servants though he was richer than Croesus.

And as he bit into his last piece of bacon, he tried not to think about anything else, even though it followed him like the London fog. Yet, uninvited, an image slipped into his mind, one that caused his heart to practically still then pick up in speed till it was painful. The one woman he actually liked. And somewhere along the way, that friendship had grown into something more.

But she didn't know that… nor would she ever. And he had a job to do today, much as he loathed the idea.

He had promised a list of eligible bachelors to her, ones that would be both dutiful and loyal to their wife. Because as much as he hated the prospect, he understood one concept far too well.

Being alone.

And he'd rather rot, rather send her into the arms of a better man than have her sentenced to the same fate as he.

# Chapter Two

MARIA KNEW THAT patience was a virtue, but the execution of said virtue was a concept she had never fully grasped. And, in her mother's opinion, that was why she talked so much. But in her defense, it was torturous to wait to see if the person with whom one was conversing would continue the conversation. It was much more dependable to maintain the flow of conversation so that there was never that deathly silence that seemed to shout *"uninteresting"* and *"spinster."* Maybe it was just she, but whenever Maria was speaking with a gentleman, she had this compulsion to continue speaking…

Thus she needed help.

Now if only that *help* would show up with a list.

Maria tapped her toe as she stared to the door, willing for Maxwell to enter the parlor with a specific card on his tray. Heaving an impatient sigh, she turned slightly to face the window. If she bent slightly to the left, she'd be able to see the street before their Town residence. Perhaps she could see if Mr. Sheppard had arrived yet?

"Maria, are you well?" Lady Moray's clipped tone broke through her search of the street.

"Pardon?" She straightened immediately, keeping her back painfully stiff from thousands of reminders permanently ingrained in her memory by her governess.

"You were listing to the side. Are you unwell?" her mother asked, enunciating each syllable as if speaking to the lesser intelligent.

Maria bit her tongue and took a calming breath through her nose. "Yes. Quite well, I assure you. I was simply admiring the view."

Her mother nodded once. "There is always the option of walking toward the window," she added with a smile.

"I'll be sure to remember that."

"My lady?" Maxwell entered the room, his emerald livery crisply pressed, and approached her mother.

"Yes?" With unhurried movements, her mother reached onto the silver platter and removed the calling card.

"A Mr. Sheppard requests a moment of Miss Maria's time."

"Finally." Maria sighed, too loudly since her mother's gaze snapped up and met hers.

"You were expecting a gentleman caller?" Her mother asked with far too much interest, serving as a reminder that gentlemen callers were few and far between.

"Er, yes." Maria nodded, keeping her decorum this time as she primly folded her hands on her lap.

"Very well." Her mother set the card back on the tray and watched as Maxwell left.

"What do we know of Mr. Sheppard?" her mother asked, her gray gaze fierce with a calculating gleam.

"He is simply a friend, Mama." Mr. Sheppard was already doing her a great service by offering suggestions for suitable husbands, and she didn't wish for him to walk into a room filled with an air of expectancy.

"They always begin as friends, my dearest," She offered with a triumphant grin.

"Oh, no. Mama truly he is just—"

"Here! Ah, Mr. Sheppard!" Her mother interrupted with a wide grin. Predatory almost.

Mr. Sheppard must have agreed because his stride into the room slowed considerably when he took in her mother. His gaze darted to her mother, then to her, then back as if second-guessing his prior promise of assistance.

Desperate, Maria stood and walked to the side, effectively blocking his retreat.

His gaze narrowed, and a light brown eyebrow arched as he gazed longingly toward the door then nodded, as if to admit defeat.

At that angle, the view of her mother was blocked, and she mouthed the word *"sorry"* as she hitched a shoulder, offering an apologetic expression — she hoped.

He shook his head once and grinned.

Relief flooded her limbs, and she relaxed slightly.

"Miss Garten, this must be your older sister." Curtis spoke to her then turned his attention to her mother.

Maria's face heated with a warm blush as she watched Curtis win over her mother with a well-placed compliment.

*The charm of a rake…*

"Aren't you the enchanter?" her mother simpered, her blush deepening slightly.

Curtis strode forward, and upon reaching her, he grasped her hand and placed a kiss to her wrist. "Only honest, my lady."

Maria shook her head slightly, completely amused. "Thank you for consenting to assist me, Mr. Sheppard."

He turned to her, taking a moment to smile mischievously before giving a quick bow. "I am always at your beck and call, Miss Garten."

"I'm sure." She only slightly resisted the urge to roll her eyes.

"Maria, why have you not told me about your entirely charming friend here? It would seem you two are on quite… familiar terms." Her mother spoke meaningfully, though a smile toyed with her lips, no doubt trying to soften the implication.

"Mr. Sheppard and I share a mutual acquaintance," Maria replied smoothly.

"Lord and Lady Langley." Mr. Sheppard supplied the names with a winning grin.

"Ah! Olivia? How delightful! How is she doing?" her mother asked. "And do please have a seat and stay a moment, Mr. Sheppard. Do you wish for tea?" Her mother was already ringing the bell before he even replied in the affirmative.

"Thank you, Lady Moray." He nodded once and sat in a wingback chair, one leg crossing over the other, completely at ease.

Lesser men would have been hightailing it through the London streets. It was well known the threat of matchmaking mamas within the *ton*, and few were as tenacious as her mother.

"To answer your question, Lord and Lady Langley are doing exceedingly wonderful."

The conversation lulled, and Maria found herself anxious to the point where her foot started to bounce impatiently. Torn, she didn't know whether to introduce another topic altogether or to just wait… proving to her mother than she could hold her tongue.

Another moment passed.

Then another.

It was too much! The silence was killing her! "Mr. Sheppard, how was your morning? I trust you had a pleasurable trip over here? How is the weather? You see, I haven't been outside as of yet, and while the window is quite helpful in ascertaining the climate, I have found that at times it is quite deceiving, and it is never a blessing to be out in the elements without a pelisse if it is colder than it appears. The sun can often make the air appear warmer—"

"Maria," her mother snapped.

The motion was repeated by Maria's mouth, and she bit her tongue.

"If you wish to have your question answered, you have to provide the opportunity for such an event…" Her mother spoke meaningfully, offering an apologetic smile in Mr. Sheppard's direction.

"Actually, Lady Moray, I find your daughter's delight in conversation to be quite invigorating. More than once, I have found myself leaving her company absolutely delighted with our discussion." He shared a glance with Maria, one that erased all the prior humiliation of her mother's scolding.

"Yes, well…" Her mother tried to begin but failed and after one moment grew into another, Mr. Sheppard addressed Maria.

"Would you be amicable to the idea of a leisurely walk through Hyde Park?"

"Of course." Maria spoke with relief, earning a slight glare from her mother.

Mr. Sheppard stood and held his arm out for Maria to take as they made the way to the door, Maria's maid discreetly following behind. "You'll be pleased to know that the weather is quite fine, Miss Garten. You'll surely want a pelisse, though I assure you that the sunshine is not casting false warmth. However, one can never be too cautious with health." He spoke softly, then a grin broke through as if he was teasing.

Maria narrowed her eyes and elbowed him slightly.

"Would your mother approve?" he asked with a mocking tone.

"Ask if I care," she dared.

Mr. Sheppard chuckled. "I must admit that your mother will forever be the icon of matchmaking mamas in my mind. When I walked into your parlor, I felt like an animal at the sales yard." He cringed slightly.

"She was rather tame, I thought," Maria replied offhandedly as she regarded the east gate to Hyde Park.

"Tame?" Mr. Sheppard paused, causing her to come to halt as well.

"Well… yes. Which, upon reflection, makes me come to two conclusions." She paused thoughtfully.

"I'm not sure I want to know."

"You, who face criminals and overly merry widows?" she retorted, daring him with a grin. "Where is your sense of adventure?"

"Why do I tell you *anything?*" he grumbled. "And I'll have you know my sense of adventure is fantastic."

She shrugged and tugged on his arm till he reluctantly began walking.

"Are you going to tell me?" he asked dubiously.

"You don't want to know," she replied, her gaze taking in a squirrel that ran across their path.

"Morbid curiosity."

"Sounds compelling."

"You have no idea."

"Very well. She either has written you off as a possible suitor because of your charming nature, or she has decided she doesn't know enough to make a conclusion, which means you'll be thoroughly investigated via her mercenary friends till she has enough information on your person to create a verdict."

As Mr. Sheppard seemed to digest her information, she studied him from the corner of her eye.

His expression was stoic, but his lips turned slightly as if fighting grin. "Well, that was unexpected."

"Not entirely. After all, you did visit an unmarried lady's house during visiting hours. She simply wasn't aware that your visit was to deliver several names of gentleman — other than yourself — eligible for her daughter." Maria replied, offering him a grin, hoping to win him over despite the prickling circumstances.

"Ah! Which reminds me." He stopped and reached into his greatcoat pocket and withdrew an envelope, no seal. "Here are several names that I believe you'll find helpful. I took the extra step and made sure that each man is secure in his own fortune, has no gambling compulsions, and is not known to be heavy-handed." He cleared his throat, his gaze direct as if trying to convey everything that wasn't said, every insinuation between the words.

"So none who will marry me for my wealth, no one who will gamble it away, and no one who will try and beat it from me?" Maria replied directly.

"Your forthrightness is at once astounding, refreshing, and slightly alarming." Mr. Sheppard asserted, as he handed over the list.

Maria took the parchment and held it tightly in her

gloved fingers, tucking it into her satchel. "Thank you."

"It was no trouble at all." He shrugged, continuing their walk.

"It was indeed trouble… and I am grateful for it." She paused and waited till he met her gaze.

"As I said… it was nothing."

"In return, I'll attempt to remove your eligibility from my mother's mental list."

"I'm afraid you'll likely find that impossible," he replied, his eyes crinkling at the edges with his grin as walked on, passing a park bench.

"Likely, but I'll do my best. Friends don't turn tail when faced with a difficulty!" She raised a fist and giggled.

"Indeed." He joined in her amusement.

As they continued, Maria felt the list a glowing coal, burning through her mind, hot with curiosity at the names written within.

"Shall we turn back?" she suggested.

"Tiring of my sparkling conversation already?" Mr. Sheppard asked, his tone wounded, though his eyes shined with mischief.

"No. But I must admit to a spectacular level of curiosity at the names you listed…" She let the implication draw out.

"Impatient?"

"Always." She grinned unrepentantly. "You knew this already, however. It comes as no surprise to you!"

"That is correct. Very well, I'll take you back to your residence and then take myself and my wounded pride elsewhere."

"I'd invite you in, but my mother—"

"Say no more…" He held up a hand and tried to restrain a mock shudder.

"She's… she means well?" Maria tried, but couldn't quite come up with the conviction in her tone necessary.

"Perhaps, but I cannot agree with the way she executes such intentions," Mr. Sheppard replied, his expression hardening slightly.

"How so?"

"Miss Garten…"

"*Maria*. We are friends, are we not?" She offered with a smile.

"Mar-ia…" He seemed to trip over the word, but she disregarded it, waiting for him to continue. "…while I am sympathetic with the difficult position the fairer sex has concerning courtship, I do not believe it is the embodiment of all that is feminine to simply be married, nor is it the highest calling a woman can have. You, as you are now, have something to offer the world, even if you are unattached at the moment. Your conversation — even one-sided — is unique, your views diverting, your laughter infections. These are not traits that will magically change or appear whether or not you marry. They're who you are. And that, my friend, is in and of itself, a wonderful and fantastic thing. Do not buy into the lie that you are a failure because no gentleman has seen fit to offer for you yet. We are a thickheaded lot." He shook his head and chuckled, reaching over and tugging on one of her bonnet strings.

Maria's heart pinched, and her eyes stung with threatening tears. "Thank you," she squeaked out, casting her gaze to the ground lest he see her lose composure.

"My dear… it's simply the truth. Now, in return for the names I provided, I have one request." He seemed to wait for her to glance up, and she did so, however reluctantly, especially as a tear splashed onto her cheek at the movement.

"Yes?"

His blue eyes were severe, warning her to take his words to heart. It was a side of him she had never seen, and for a moment, she wondered just how deep the unknown mystery of Curtis Sheppard ran. "Remember what I said. And *when* you marry…" He emphasized the word, making her heart soften. "…marry for love, for the joy of living together, for the hope of the future you'll make. Don't marry to simply feel wanted. I assure you that even marriage can be lonely. Don't settle for anything less than heaven on earth. Please."

"Of course," she answered, never once expecting to marry for less than love, yet at the same time, never realizing she had put it as such a priority either.

"Thank you." His shoulders sagged slightly, as if unloading a heavy burden.

Maria regarded him, studying his features. She was tempted to ask more, to ask how he knew about the loneliness of marriage — he, a confirmed bachelor — but restrained as she noticed a shift in his gaze.

"And this is where I live up to my legend." He turned his gaze back to her, his eyes bright with intelligence. "Huffton!" he called out, raising a hand in greeting.

Turning, Maria noticed a gentleman walking through the park on his blood bay gelding. The gentleman paused and offered a smile to Mr. Sheppard then approached them. After dismounting, he dipped a slight bow to her.

"And what brings you out and about on this fine day, my friend?" Huffton asked Mr. Sheppard, yet his gaze remained on her.

"Taking the air with a friend. Let me introduce you to my lovely companion. Lord Huffton, this is Miss Garten."

"Your servant, Miss Garten." The gentleman bowed,

kissing her wrist lightly, leaving a tingling sensation where his lips brushed her skin.

"The pleasure is mine, Lord Huffton," she replied, studying the man before her. He wasn't overly tall, but was easily several inches above her stature. Soft brown curls crowned his head and matched the friendly hue to his brown eyes. Immediately, she felt comfortable with his acquaintance.

"I was just commenting on my displeasure at needing to cut our friendly amble short. More's the pity since it is such a lovely day…" Mr. Sheppard let the words linger.

"It is indeed a lovely day," Lord Huffton affirmed, "and a pity to cut short anytime with so lovely a lady."

"Indeed. Would you perhaps be inclined to see Miss Garten home? I'm afraid to be late to my next appointment and would be forever in your debt," Mr. Sheppard asked, his expression pleading yet also regretful.

Maria made a mental note to ask him about his ability to act later. Surely he was quite adept at it.

"I'd be honored," Lord Huffton replied immediately, his grin growing as he turned to Maria once more.

"Thank you," she coquetted — rather, she *hoped* she did.

"I'll leave you two then. Thank you!" And with a jaunty wave, Mr. Sheppard walked off, hands in his pockets, and quickly disappeared down the path.

"Shall we?" Lord Huffton extended his arm, a smile on his face. Accepting his hand, she strode beside him as his fine animal followed their lead. She'd have to thank Mr. Sheppard later, and she wondered if Lord Huffton's name was on the list.

Knowing Mr. Sheppard, Lord Huffton indeed was. The thought sent a smile to her lips as she walked with one of the men who just may end up being… more.

# Chapter Three

**C**URTIS CLENCHED HIS jaw as he strode from Huffton and Maria, her soft laughter following him as each step sealed her fate, and sealed his own. He was a mad man to hand deliver her to another man's arms… his bed. The thought made his blood race with a fury, yet he suppressed the desire to turn about and make a cake of himself. Rather, he placed one foot in front of the other and walked away.

He had plans for the day; he'd not be deterred by bell-like laughter and a woman that could talk his ear off. As he made his way through the gate and toward the Garten residence where his carriage awaited, he pondered her mother's actions. Truly, he had felt a shiver a dread when he met Lady Moray. The woman gave the word *predator* a face, and he was all too familiar with the intentions dancing in her gaze; yet what he couldn't forget was the way she disregarded her daughter. Maria had confided in him once, telling him that her mother had claimed the reason she was unmarried was her inability to keep silent. Yet to a man, where silence was worse than the pox, he rather adored her incessant chatter. Although he had noticed that it only made an appearance when she was far too nervous to think through her thoughts before speaking, that wasn't a detriment to her personality, rather a lovely faucet that illuminated a sharp wit and sensible humor.

He signaled to his coachman as he approached, and the man dismounted and opened the door for him to enter the conveyance. "Home." He said the word, knowing that the meaning and the sensation of it were two very separate things, yet that was his truth, his sentence, his future.

The only thing waiting for him was a snifter of brandy and perhaps a new assignment. Expelling a heavy sigh, he tapped the roof of the carriage three times, knowing it would signal the driver to change destinations. How in heaven's name had it come to this? As the conveyance made a turn and headed toward the residence of Lord and Lady Langley, Curtis gave a humorless laugh. The Forsaken Lord was now anything but, as he and his lovely wife had one heir and a spare on the way, the house once deserted by any joy, now was overflowing.

The carriage halted in front of the large stone residence, and before he even alighted, the butler had the residence door open and an eyebrow quirked.

"Tell me, Winston, what is the news today?" Curtis asked, a grin pulling at his lips as the butler very uncharacteristically rolled his eyes.

"I do believe Lord Langley will need another decanter of brandy."

"Ah, did he drink it all?" Curtis asked, shrugging out of his coat.

"No," Winston answered with a pinched grin.

"And you'll not disclose the story?" Curtis asked, his curiosity piqued.

"I believe it is best… seen." Winston nodded in the direction of the Langley's study, and Curtis glanced back and forth between the door and the butler, hesitant.

Especially as he heard shouting.

But as laughter echoed after the shouting, he started in the direction of the sound. The heavy wooden door was already slightly open, and he pressed on the dark wood, causing it to swing gently inward. The sight that greeted his eyes was almost overwhelming — and exactly what he needed to distract him.

Two maids swept up the shattered remains of a decanter, while another mopped up the… brandy, judging from the strong aroma in the room. His gaze took in a smoldering hearth broom, its bristles almost burnt off as it rested on the stone next to the fireplace. The scent of smoke contended with the sweet and tangy fragrance of the brandy. Another maid was beating one of the heavy curtains next to Langley's desk, and he noticed smoke swirling about as she did so.

What in heaven's name had happened here? As his gaze swept the room, he noticed Langley sitting in a chair, three-year-old Thomas beside him. The poor lad was wiping his nose as tears slid down his young face.

Curtis was about to speak when he heard footsteps in the hall and turned to find Lady Langley approaching, her lips pursed as if trying to suppress laughter.

"Do I dare ask?" Curtis asked as she noticed his presence.

"If you can keep a straight face, yes. If you can't, I'll tell you later," she murmured quickly as she entered the room and approached her husband and son. "Here, Thomas." She placed a cool cloth to the child's face, wiping off some of the soot that smudged on his cheek.

Langley rubbed his face with his hands, as if fighting inwardly. "Don't even start, Curtis. I beg you." He spoke in articulate tones.

"Very well." He rocked on his heels, sniffing, trying to relieve the way his nose stuffed up from the smoke in the room.

"I'm s-so sorr-y." Thomas tried to say as he wiped his nose once more, sniffling.

Curtis' heart softened toward the clearly repentant lad. Poor guy had clearly been through a lot, probably self-imposed, but quite a bit regardless!

"I know, son…" Langley replied, his tone tired yet kind.

Tenderly, the once reclusive and dangerous lord reached out and pulled the little copy of himself into a tight hug, resting his head atop of his son's. Curtis glanced away, his heart heavy with the knowledge that he'd never know the affection — or devastation — of a three-year-old heir.

Amongst the *ton*, children were seen as a means to an end, a necessary evil for their titles to live on. Taught to be neither seen nor heard, the children were usually raised by a governess or servant. Curtis was thankful to see that Langley and Olivia didn't adhere to the status quo.

And if he were a different man, he wouldn't either.

But there were some things one couldn't change.

"You mustn't ever try to drink your father's brandy." Olivia spoke quietly.

"And if you do spill, do not use the hearth broom to try and clean it," Langley added.

"Or put it back near the fire." Olivia placed her hands on her hips.

"Yes, Mama." Thomas nodded once, his little body shaking.

"And if something does catch fire, do *not* try to put it out by waving it around." Langley speared his son with a direct gaze.

"Especially if there are other things that can catch fire."

"I un-understand." The boy sobbed slightly.

"But there was no one hurt, and that is what is most important," his mother added.

Curtis simply watched as the family worked together, correcting and growing, a beautiful example of what a home should be like — minus the smoke.

"Now, run along and play. And please do not come in my office unless invited. Are we understood?" Langley waited till Thomas nodded once and turned to leave the room.

As the lad passed, Curtis reached out and smoothed the child's mop of curly dark hair, marveling at its soft texture. Offering Thomas a grin, he was encouraged as the boy started to skip then run down the hall toward the stairs.

"One day…" Langley stood and dusted off his hands, his gaze taking in the disarray of his once-immaculate study.

"One day?" Curtis asked, ambling into the room.

"One day you'll know the joy and terror of a little miniature Curtis Sheppard. And I'll glory in the destruction it causes to both your sanity and heart." He chuckled and shook his head.

"Ah, yes. Not likely. The world cannot handle two of me. Would be unfair on females everywhere." He joked about it, keeping his demeanor carefree and light.

"Still the confirmed bachelor?" Olivia asked, her regard sharper than her husband's.

"Afraid so. All the worthy ladies are spoken for." He shrugged his shoulders as if disappointed.

"None of that," Langley growled, glaring at Curtis.

Curtis wagged his eyebrows at him.

"Not any better," Langley grumbled, rubbing the back of his neck as he studied the dying fire in the hearth. "What brings you here? Not that I'm opposed to your dropping in uninvited." He glanced to him, a knowing expression in his eyes.

Curtis grinned. He had long ago ceased following any sort of protocol when it came to his friend, Langley. Of course, that was back when he was concerned about the sanity of said friend due to his reclusive state, but when Olivia re-entered his life… that was the beginning of an awakening of sorts for the cynical lord.

Odd how things changed, yet stayed the same. Here he was, visiting the one place that used to house the forsaken, all because he felt too lonely to be at his own residence.

He disregarded the pathetic thought.

He paced about the room, sidestepping a singed piece of curtain. "Can't I simply drop by to bless you with my presence?"

"If your presence was a blessing," Langley retorted, sharing a smile with his wife.

He gave a broad sweep of his hand.

"We all know that it is. I light up a room simply by being in it."

"Pity I can't see the light."

"Too much smoke."

"Of course." Langley rolled his eyes.

"If you two will play nice, I'll leave you be and send Winston up with tea." Lady Langley shook her head as a smile graced her lips. After a squeeze to her husband's shoulder, she walked toward the door.

Langley's gaze followed her with a heat that could have easily made the room catch fire once more.

"Careful, you'll singe your wife with that smolder," Curtis harassed Langley as he walked toward the window, gazing outside at the quiet Mayfair Street.

"Jealousy will get you nowhere," Langley replied with an amused tone. "So, why are you really here?"

Curtis rose from his chair, making wide strides across the carpeted floor, only to pause beside him, speaking lowly. "I uncovered some information of Lord Whittle's involvement with Craysen."

"And?"

"He was not involved as much as we anticipated. There's another third party that is, rather, was initiating the trade. Whittle was an expendable middleman."

"A rather expensive middleman. His loyalty must have been purchased and with his deep pockets. It must have been quite a sum," Langley added, his tone curious.

"Indeed, if money was the type of payment." Curtis closed his eyes, hating that he saw the dark side of London, the dark side of human nature.

"What are you saying?" Langley turned, facing him.

Curtis slowly slid his gaze from the street to his friend.

"As it turns out, there was a family estate brought into question… an inheritance. Crayson understood that Whittle knew intimate details concerning the family's current state…"

"And one trade was made for another…"

"And when the family in question had deep pockets and deeper connections than anticipated…"

"I see. Crayson was expendable because there was a bigger fish to catch, so to say."

"Exactly."

"So…" Langley rocked on his heels. "…what is the next step?"

Curtis exhaled a deep breath. "The family was already

vaguely aware of the situation and took matters into their own hands. A, shall we say, interested gentleman took it upon himself to see to the heiress' welfare."

"One of *our* gentlemen?" Langley speared him with a look.

"Yes. Neville."

He nodded approvingly. "Good man."

"One of the best… aside from myself, that is," Curtis added with a smirk.

"Present company always excluded." Langley gave a quick nod.

"So, we wait. He will send word once he has information."

Langley groaned. "How I hate the wait."

"You never were the patient sort. Always worked against you in the field."

"And you, who are known for your saint-like patience," he replied with heavy sarcasm.

Curtis shrugged and walked away from the window. "Amongst other alarmingly brilliant qualities."

"Curtis?" Langley's voice halted him, and he turned and waited.

"All joking aside, I know just how patient you can be… and it's lethal. But I have to wonder if that trait also works against you." Langley didn't turn from the window but let his words hang, swirling with meaning like wind-spun fog.

"I'm sure I don't know what you mean." Curtis' jaw flexed as he took a step toward the door.

"Patience is not always a virtue. Rather, denial isn't. I never thought I'd see the day when I was lecturing you on love."

Curtis could hear Langley's footsteps approach him. His feet itched to made large strides to the door.

"Truly, it is an odd twist of fate that you'd take such a hopeless venture upon your shoulders." Curtis turned to offer this friend an easy grin, no matter how his jaw ached from being clenched.

"Olivia and I watched you last night. Does Miss Maria have any clue of your regard for her?" Langley paused, placing his hands in his pockets and regarding his friend with a piercing gaze.

"Miss *Garten* and I are simply friends. You're imagining things in your old age."

"I imagined nothing of the sort. And we are back to the issue of denial. It will get you nowhere with me since I am quite convinced of the truth. It will save us much time and effort if you'll simply be honest with me… and yourself." Langley walked over to a wingback chair and sat.

Irritated, Curtis very much wanted to punch the patiently tolerant expression from his face.

But he restrained himself, barely.

"Again, I have no idea—"

"You watched her for at least a quarter hour before you approached her. Each time she would laugh, you'd smile. Each time she'd glance to a potential suitor, you'd narrow your eyes and flex your hands. When she'd move on, you'd relax till it finally was too much for you to simply watch. You had to interact, to hear her voice, dance with her. You counted the dances till the waltz then approached her, making it look like happenstance."

"Bloody hell," Curtis swore then strode to a chair and slumped in its embrace. "Sometimes I hate you."

Langley chuckled. "I assure you, the feeling is entirely mutual."

Curtis glared at his friend. "Your powers of observation

are monumental, but they don't mean I'm going to act on whatever you feel you've uncovered in my little black heart." He gave a wry grin to his friend.

"Why?" Langley leaned forward, resting his elbows on his knees.

"Why?" Curtis snorted. "Because—" He stopped himself. "—because." And nodded once.

"How persuading." Langley rolled his eyes as he stood and walked to the sideboard, where he pulled out two glasses and filled them with brandy. "If I'm to listen to your lies, I'll have to be relaxed so that I do not throttle you." He gave a sarcastic grin.

"What do you want me to say Langley? That I pine for her? That I—" He took a dramatic sniff. "—I wish that she loved me and only me for the rest of time and eternity?"

"Now you're simply being an ass. An overly dramatic one. Don't embarrass yourself."

Curtis accepted the glass Langley handed him and took a sip of the slightly sweet and acidic liquid. "French?"

"Shhh."

"Nothing like it." He took another sip.

"Let me start you." Langley took a seat and cleared his throat. "I am afraid of pursing Miss Garten because…" He made a sweeping gesture with his hand and waited for his friend to finish.

Curtis rolled his eyes. "I'm not afraid."

"You're something."

"I'm… being the better man." He nodded and took a sip as if rewarding himself.

Langley's brows knit in confusion. "How so?"

Curtis took a long breath. "She deserves a marriage that is the fulfillment of her feminine fantasies All I know about marriage is how to slowly kill your spouse via betrayal and verbal sparring." He lifted his glass in a self-congratulatory toast.

"And you are incapable of being a better man than your father?" Langley asked sagely.

"I do not…" He took a breath then started again. "I do not trust myself to be the caliber of man that I want her to have."

"I see." Langley sat back, his expression thoughtful.

"Which is why I have already given her a list of suitors who would include the type of man she needs."

Langley started to sputter, choking on the sip of brandy he had just taken. "Pardon?" he asked between coughs.

"She asked for assistance. Her horrific mother has done nothing but create a deep-seated insecurity within her, and she feels she'll never be married and firmly on the shelf." He shrugged. "She deserves to be loved… so I selected several gentlemen without vices who would be good candidates."

Langley blinked. "You've gone mad."

"No. I've thought it through."

"No, I do not think you have." Langley stood and walked to the cabinet once more. "This is taking more brandy than I anticipated." He filled his glass once more. "You do realize that when she marries another man, she will no longer dance with you, entertain you with her sparkling conversation and wit, amongst other things?"

"I understand." Curtis nodded, though his chest tightened with each word Langley said.

"Have you considered that maybe… just maybe… she wants *you*? Rather than a different gentleman?" Langley swirled the brandy in his glass as he spoke.

Curtis paused. He actually hadn't considered that facet.

Could she? No. Certainly not. He had never given her anything but friendship.

"Would you lead her in a different direction… with a different man… when the possibility exists that who she wants… is you? And if so, have you considered that you are pushing her in the same direction that your mother was pushed? So, the argument you presented for not pursing her is actually the very argument for you to actually reverse your previous statement and pay her court?"

Curtis blinked. "That… was quite the running dialogue."

"I'll simplify." Langley set his glass down. "Your reasoning for not pursing her is bloody wretched, and you need to grow a pair of bollocks and do something."

Curtis glanced to the Aubusson rug. Could Langley be right? If… if Miss Maria did have some sort of affection for him, and he pushed her away — especially when his heart was likewise invested — was he only propitiating what happened in his parents' marriage? The very thing he was desperately trying to avoid?

"I'm bloody damned either way," he muttered, looking the situation from every direction.

Langley walked over and slapped him on the back once, hard. "Welcome to love."

"But, I mean, I already gave her the list…" He ran his fingers through his hair, his mind spinning.

"And she's already spoken for?" Langley asked.

"No."

"Then get off your ass and do something. Seriously. My son catches on quicker than you, and he's a tot!"

"So what do I do?" Curtis glanced up, a fierce hope and desperation pounding in his chest.

"You're brilliant. You'll figure it out." Langley shrugged.

"But may I suggest that you start now rather than later?"

"Right." Curtis stood, his brow furrowed as he thought through several scenarios.

But none of them worked.

Because… well, he didn't want to just pursue her. He wanted to win.

But only if she was already invested.

But how to tell if she was? It was a dilemma.

"Curtis?" Langley's voice brought him back from his deep thought.

"Yes?"

"Go. You'll figure it out, but may I make a suggestion?"

"Of course."

"Make it grand. Don't be stingy on the very thing that is based on generosity. Love."

Curtis nodded. With a final wave, he quit the room and was soon out the door and in his carriage. He instructed the driver to simply amble about, giving him time to think. As Bond Street came into view, he spotted a small shop that boasted specialized paper and secretarial supplies.

And a thought pelted him like a snowball.

He quickly tapped the roof, and the driver pulled over to the side of the cobbled street.

With a grin and more hope than he'd experienced in his previous thirty-one years, he crossed the busy street and made an important purchase.

One he hoped would change everything.

# Chapter Four

"What do you mean you do not know who sent it?" Lady Moray narrowed her gray eyes skeptically.

Maria blinked at the beautiful array of red tulips with bright yellow centers, delivered just a few moments ago. "To say this is unexpected is an understatement." She ran a gloved finger along the deep green stem opening to a bright red flower.

"And there was no note?" Her mother's voice broke through her admiration.

"Not that I noticed," Maria answered, distracted by the lovely, colorful petals. "But my, aren't they lovely?" She inhaled deeply, the scent light and reminiscent of spring.

"Well… this is simply not done." Her mother sniffed delicately, but from the corner of Maria's eye, she could see a smile at her mother's lips.

"Then why are you smiling?" she asked cheekily.

"Because you, my dear, have a secret admirer. A suitor." With a wink, her mother left in a murmur of pale yellow muslin.

"An admirer," Maria breathed the words, tasting the delicious flavor of them. But who could it be? Was this a gift from Lord Huffton? Likely not, but there was always a chance, wasn't there?

She studied the blooms then glanced to the box that had conveyed them from the florist to her doorstep. Had she missed the note? Or perhaps it had been dropped on the way to delivery? She lifted the damp paper lining the box but came up empty. Surely, whoever sent the flowers wished some sort of recognition.

Why else offer a gift to a lady?

Unless… unless he didn't want their intentions to be taken wrong.

Eyes narrowing, she studied the flowers once more. Tulips. Not roses, not an array of blooms that would convey a secret message, just beautiful tulips.

Biting her, lip, she wondered. Would Mr. Sheppard do such a thing? He had been quite sympathetic in the park when discussing her mother. Was he simply trying to cheer her up?

By not enclosing a note, he would remain unnamed and absent from her mother's list of eligible bachelors.

Truly, it was the only reasonable explanation for such a beautiful and anonymous gift.

Yet, even as she considered the possibility, it seemed unlikely.

And oddly enough, she rather liked the idea of a secret admirer. It was deeply romantic. What woman wouldn't appreciate such knowledge?

With a smile, she signaled a footman and had him pick up the flowers, follow her to her room, then place them on her writing desk. With a nod of dismissal, the footman left her alone with the bouquet.

A knock on the door startled her. "Miss Garten? A missive

arrived for you from a Miss Rebecca Lockett." Maxwell, their long-time family butler, displayed the cream-colored envelope on a silver plate.

"A Miss Lockett?" Maria strode across the room and lifted the envelope, studying the name. "Thank you." She dismissed Maxwell and furrowed her brow as she studied the name. Never had she heard of a Miss Rebecca Lockett. Perhaps she was new this Season? Or some relation? It was quite odd to receive a missive from an unknown, yet her curiosity kept her from simply setting it on her desk and forgetting about it. Rather, she took out an erasing knife to open the wax seal. The thick paper then opened gently and revealed a single folded sheet. She set the envelope down and opened the parchment.

> *Miss Garten,*
>
> *I hope this letter finds you well. Did you enjoy the tulips? I find them a beautiful herald of spring. I must also confess to using a bit of a ruse to get this letter to you, as I'm sure you have figured there is no Rebecca Lockett.*

Maria's frown deepened as she sat in her desk chair and continued reading.

> *I realize I am bending the social conventions that state a gentleman should never give written contact to a lady he is not promised to; however, I hope you'll forgive my forward nature. I'm afraid I cannot hide that aspect of my character. Nor can I hide my candid way of speaking, even in letter form. So, remaining true to that*

*nature, I simply wish to tell you that you are beautiful. Your smile is a highlight of each day that I'm blessed to see it, and I could listen to your amusing conversation for hours on end. I wish to get to know you better without the... tedious nature of ballroom conversation. If you're willing to take such a risk, simply leave the bouquet of tulips in a window, visible from the street.*

*If you do not, then please simply enjoy the gift from a sincere heart. I wish you all the best.*

*Hopefully yours*

Maria set the letter on her desk, her eyes straying to it then focusing as she thought through all that was stated. Well, she was now certain that she had an admirer! But... whether she was excited about the prospect was now a bit more confusing. What if the gentleman in question was an older gentleman, a grandfatherly one who knew she'd never consider him? Or perhaps some other unsavory scandal or situation that he wished to keep hidden from her till she was somewhat attached?

Her mind spun with possibilities. It was indeed odd that whoever it was didn't want to adhere to social conventions. Was that a good or bad thing? Honestly, she didn't know.

But she had to make a choice.

She studied the tulips once more, contemplating.

What was the harm in progressing? She could see no ill consequences should she accept the challenge laid out in the letter. Rather, the rewards were far greater than the risk.

So, with a deep breath, she lifted the vase and walked

from her room. After carefully navigating the stairs, she paused, her gaze darting between the green parlor and the library, both with windows facing the street. With a step toward the library, she halted her steps and turned to the parlor. A round table was already positioned by the window. She placed the flowers on the table, careful to gently move the books currently resting there. Tilting her head, she studied the angle. With a twist to her lips, she walked to the front door and took the steps down to the street. Her skirts swished, and she spun and searched the window for the flowers. Sure enough, they were clearly seen from the street. With a decisive nod, she returned to her house and marched up the stairs. Now, to simply wait.

She only wished she knew exactly for whom she was waiting.

# Chapter Five

CURTIS DELAYED A tormenting thirty-five minutes before he knocked on the door. After all, he wanted to be sure that he played his hand correctly. Being overeager wouldn't work in his favor, but being apathetic wouldn't help either.

It was a delicate balance.

So, after he ordered the flowers and wrote the note under the phony name, he'd taken a position in the park allowing him a direct view of the house, but not in plain sight so as to be discovered.

His heart hammered as the bright red and yellow tulips lit up the window's view. And when Maria exited the house and stood in front, evaluating the view of the tulips, he stifled a chuckle.

How like her.

Which was all the more endearing, and all the more affirming that he was taking the correct course of action.

When enough time had passed, he approached her door and was thankfully escorted directly into their parlor.

"Lady Moray will be with you shortly." The old butler bowed then left him to wait.

Without hesitation, he strode to the window and

removed the flowers from their perch on the table, choosing to place them as far out of sight as possible. He bit back a grin as he anticipated Maria's response.

Just as he found a suitable location, Lady Moray entered, offering him a questioning gaze and polite greeting.

"Good afternoon, Mr. Sheppard." She folded her hands neatly and raised a brow.

"Lovely afternoon, Lady Moray." He gave a jaunty bow and a quick grin, noticing how she blushed slightly but held a firm gaze.

"I'm under the assumption that you are here to visit my daughter?" She cut directly to the point.

"Indeed."

"And may I ask what your intentions are?" Her gaze was spearing, as if trying to lift the answer from his mind.

"You may certainly ask." He shrugged. "Your daughter is a dear friend, and I have a dilemma with a current situation that I find her insight is necessary in solving."

"You realize that this is highly peculiar for the opposite sexes to have such a… plutonic friendship." She tilted her chin slightly, watching him.

"You have no need to worry—" He broke off when he heard footsteps in the hall signaling Maria's entrance. Her mother smoothed her skirt and turned on a beaming smile.

He expected to see Maria and feel a genuine affection. He expected her hair to be that familiar golden-honey color that brought out the green of her eyes. He expected her dress to be cut to better define her already beautiful figure.

What he did not expect was to be rendered speechless. Nor was he expecting for his stomach to wrap itself in fisherman's knots or his palms to grow damp.

Bloody hell, what was wrong with him?

On the outside, he held a firm grasp of his demeanor.

On the inside, he was a coming apart at the seams.

It was damn terrifying.

Electrifying.

Addicting.

And never had he wanted her more.

Because he had inadvertently discovered just how much he wanted her to begin with. Not for a night, not for a season…

But forever.

And before this whole bloody escapade even started, he had been able to lie to himself well enough that he'd believed he would be all right without her.

And the danger about lying to oneself was that, with time, the lie was believed.

And he had.

Until now.

Now, everything was different, and he had not a bloody clue as to what to do next.

"Mr. Sheppard? Mr. Sheppard!" Her clear eyes took on a confused expression before smoothing out into a welcoming smile.

He offered her a friendly grin, one he knew she would recognize. "Good day, Miss Garten."

"What a lovely surprise," she added, her cheer growing more genuine and giving him far more hope than he'd expected.

"I am a man of many talents, surprise being one of them." He shrugged, and like a magnet, he walked toward her, drawn.

"Many, many talents," she teased, her green eyes dancing. Yet her gaze shifted from him to the window, and he saw her eyes widen.

*Ah. She'd noticed.*

Maria took a quick breath as if to speak then obviously thought better of it, closing her lips tightly and offering a polite smile, even as her eyes darted from his and back to where the flowers should have been before scanning the room. When she spotted the blooms in their relocated place, her eyes widened, and she started toward them.

"Mother, why did you move my lovely tulips? They need sunshine." Her tone was light, but she made quick work of picking up the vase and moving the flowers to their original position.

"Why, dear, I did not move them," Lady Moray answered, understandably confused. "I do not see how it matters either way, however." She waved her gloved hand dismissively.

Maria gave a short huff. "Of course it matters! Simple botany."

Curtis watched with amusement as she set the flowers down and carefully arranged them, angling them just right. Biting back a grin, he simply couldn't resist the temptation of wreaking a bit of havoc on Maria.

"Actually, upon entering the parlor, I noticed the tulips and moved them out of the sunlight. It's dreadfully warm this season, and I didn't want such lovely blooms to wilt." He shrugged. He bit his cheek to keep from smiling as he walked over, lifted the vase, and started walking across the room to put it on the far table once more.

"But, you can't..." Maria followed him, yet he persisted.

"Maria, if Mr. Sheppard is of the persuasion that your beloved tulips need less sun, perhaps you should listen to him. After all, you'll want such a thoughtful gift to last..." Her mother drew out the words, offering just enough information to create curiosity, should he find himself wondering.

*Well played.*

"A gift?" He took the bait willingly, standing between the tulips and Maria, grinning at her as she glared.

"Yes," she answered, placing her hands on her hips. "My gift. Meaning, I can put them wherever I wish," she retorted without heat, simply irritation as she tried to step around him, yet he continued to foil her attempts.

"From whom?" he asked, curious as to how she'd answer.

"There was no note," her mother replied.

Curtis glanced to Lady Moray and smiled his thanks.

"Ah, so it's a secret gift. From perhaps… an admirer?" Only through years of training was he able to force his expression to be impassive with just a hint of interest. It was a particularly useful expression, one he'd learned to use over the years. Yet even as he waited, his heart hammered.

"I do not think it is any of your concern," Maria shot back, eyes narrowing. Then she quickly faked a sidestep, and when he fell for it, she deftly went around him, lifted the vase, and started back toward the window.

Her persistence pleased him.

Would she be as determined if she knew who had sent them?

"Since they are your gift, you should most certainly choose where they will be displayed." He gave in, having enjoyed the short game.

"Why, thank you, Mr. Sheppard," Maria did not bother to glance back but arranged the vase once more and glanced out the window.

"Care for a walk?" Curtis asked, seizing the opportunity to escape the watchful eye of her mother.

"I suppose," she answered absentmindedly.

"Maria! Is that anyway to answer a gentleman?" Lady Moray's tone was especially strident, and he saw Maria jump slightly.

"Forgive me. I find I'm terribly distracted. Mr. Sheppard, I would be honored to take a walk with you. I'm in desperate need of fresh air." She turned a beaming smile to him, one that had every last thought fleeing from his mind.

He stammered. "Well, that is... shall we?" He cleared his throat and offered his arm.

"Of course." She took it and walked toward the parlor's exit.

"I'll send along Maybell with you," her mother called.

Sure enough, just as they started down the stairs leading from her house, a quiet maid started to follow at a reasonable distance.

"So... a gift? Flowers, no less... and you have no idea from whom?" He attempted to keep his expression only slightly interested.

She gave him a sidelong glance. "Yes."

He waited for her to elaborate.

As the moment stretched into two, he bit his tongue, trying to keep from prodding her for more information.

True to her nature, his patience paid off.

"The secret is killing me," she gushed out, as if having held in the words like air and finally releasing them. "To not know... yet it's this delicious secret! An admirer? How romantic. It's like the Gothic novels I'm supposed to never read!"

He grinned, taking in her exuberant expressions and the way her eyes lit up with hope as she spoke.

"Very Gothic and romantic." He nodded, secretly pleased

with her assessment.

They crossed a street and entered Hyde Park. "Can you keep a secret?" she murmured, her gaze darting to meet his then turning back toward the green-lined path.

He placed his hand over his heart, pretending to be wounded. "I'm hurt. Truly, you felt the need to ask such a thing?"

"This is not just any secret," she scolded, playfully smacking him. "This is truly a keep-it-locked-up secret."

"Locked up?"

"Yes. As in, be a vault." She paused, hands on her luscious hips as her pertinent expression teased him.

He made a locking motion with his hand over his mouth then pretended to throw away the key.

To which she rolled her eyes. "Clever. But throwing away the key is foolish. You're to hand it back to the person who gave you the secret. Then she is the one who can tell you when to unlock such secret knowledge."

"You've put some thought into this."

"Indeed," she answered then waited.

Enchanted, he made another locking motion and handed her the pretend key.

"Thank you." She nodded once and started walking.

"And the secret?" he questioned as they made their way toward the Serpentine.

"In a minute. There are entirely too many people."

As he glanced around them, he blinked. "I count four," he replied softly.

"Four too many," she answered immediately.

"I see." He tried to hold back a chuckle but failed, earning him a glare.

She took a side path that led away from the blue-green

water and into a more wooded, less-populated area. "Over here." She nodded toward the trees.

"Your wish is my command." He followed dutifully, his face aching with the struggle of holding back a wide grin. He didn't want her to get the impression that he thought her silly. Rather, he was fully charmed by a new quirk in her already dazzling personality. Truly, life with Maria would never be dull… or silent.

How had he never seen such a perfect fit before?

"Now…" She sighed, folding her hands in front of her and turning to face him. "…you must not say a word."

"Haven't we already discussed this? I gave you my key." He nodded sagely.

"True, but one can never be too certain."

He held up a hand. "I pledge my secret keeping."

"Very good."

"So…" He gave an impatient grin.

"So… I…" She took a breath. "…I received a letter."

When she didn't continue, he asked, "From whom?"

"A Miss Rebecca Lockett."

"Pardon? Your admirer is a woman?" He blinked, pretending shock.

"No! Heavens, no. It's a gentleman sending me a letter under the guise of a lady named Rebecca Lockett. There is no Rebecca Lockett," she gushed out in a quick sentence.

"Oh, I see." He took a step to the side, pacing a bit. "And what did the letter say?"

Her white teeth bit down on her lower pink lip, accentuating the plump shape of it, distracting him fully, and making blood rush to all the wrong places.

At least the wrong places for the moment.

"It was an introduction—"

"So he gave you his name?" he interrupted, trying to distract himself.

"No, no… just stated his intentions." She nodded firmly.

"Which are?"

"To get to know me… without the constraints of ballroom conversation."

He smiled to himself at her direct quote. "Was that all the letter said?"

"No, he revealed that he had a difficult time adhering to polite society's rule structure, which I think most men tend to find difficult, regardless. As a woman, I find it difficult at times. That wasn't a shocking revelation." She shrugged. "Oh, and he said that if I was willing to converse with him… get to know him better… I only had to put the tulips in a window visible from the street. He'd take that as a signal."

He ceased his pacing, grinning at her. "So that's why you fought so fiercely when I tried to move them!"

"You truly were relentless! I couldn't believe you moved them," she replied, as if remembering her frustration.

"I? Relentless? You were bound and determined to put them back in the window! And now I know why. Say, do you think he's seen them?" Curtis asked, leaning forward slightly.

"I haven't a clue. I hope." Her eyes widened.

"When did you receive them?"

"Today."

He gave a quick laugh. "I know that, but what time of the day?"

"Oh, this morning around ten, I believe. The letter came about a half hour later. And I moved them to the window immediately after reading the note."

"He's seen them." Curtis gave a firm nod.

She eyed him skeptically. "How can you be so sure?"

"This was clearly planned. He was surely waiting."

"Are you certain?"

"Yes."

"Oh my." She lifted a gloved hand to her lips, her eyes growing unfocused as she looked right through him. "What do I do now?" Her gaze sharpened.

Curtis was enjoying the conversation far more than he'd expected. It was delightful to be on the inside and know… to watch her reactions and be the one to temper them as well. He only hoped that *when* the truth came about, she'd forgive him.

Of course, if she were reluctant, he could always… persuade her.

He grinned at the thought, his body tightening with the implication.

"Well?" Maria's voice broke through his musing, and he cleared his throat, hoping it would help to clear his head.

"Well, I'd imagine he'd make the next move." Curtis shrugged.

Her shoulders sagged. "So I have to just wait?"

"Don't look so dejected. I'm sure he won't make you wait long," he encouraged, but when her countenance didn't improve, he couldn't resist reaching out and tipping her chin upward. At the first brush of her skin against his fingers, his body responded. It was different. Just as he'd experienced earlier in the parlor, this new awakening — rather acceptance — of his regard for her was inflicting bloody havoc on his entire body. Hadn't he held her countless times during a waltz? Wasn't that far more intimate than a swift touch? Yet, it didn't feel that way.

Damn it all, those bloody feelings were going to be the death of him. Rather, they were going to tell her the truth far sooner than he was ready to admit. So, not long after he lifted her chin upward, he removed his hand, ignoring the way it tingled and ached to touch her again.

"You just wait and see," he whispered, unable to do more.

Her lips parted, green eyes shifted back and forth studying him, and he quickly closed of his expression, lest he be exposed.

"Truly." He spoke with a forced light tone.

She shook her head once, as if clearing it. "I'll believe you, but if you're proven wrong, I'm blaming you for the chocolate I'll be eating." A twitch of a grin toyed with her lips and then bloomed across her face.

"Fair's fair." He shrugged, enjoying the delight of her smile.

"Very well." She glanced behind him. "Would it be terribly rude of me to ask you to take me back home? Just in case?" She bit her lip once more, an anxious yet excited expression in her eyes.

"I'm hurt. Clearly I've been replaced with a letter," Curtis answered, his tone wounded even as he smirked.

"It is hard to compete with the written word. Many a war has been fought over letters. Many a lady has been won," she quipped.

"Indeed, indeed." Curtis held out his arm, and as she took it. He led them back toward the Serpentine with the intention of heading back to her residence. "As aptly as you put that, I must add one caveat." He slid a glance to her.

"Oh?"

"Letters are just that… letters. Words rearranged to give an intended meaning. What is most important is why the letters were written. The intention. Because I assure you, no war, no lady has been won, no monumental event has ever happened because of the words alone, but because of the truth behind them."

The only sound in the pregnant silence was the few birds twittering the branches above them as they passed the cool green water and onto the path toward the park exit.

"Do you always have to be so wildly intelligent?" she finally answered, cutting a glance to him.

He nodded. "Yes. Yes, I do."

"It's quite annoying. However, you are right," she admitted, albeit reluctantly.

"I know."

She arched a brow. "And humble."

"Always."

"And I might need to… to… I don't know… do something to take away from that lethal charm."

"It's called confidence." He wagged an eyebrow, enjoying their verbal sparring.

"You have too much."

"You can never have enough."

She tilted her head slightly. "I beg to differ."

"And I graciously disagree."

"Then we are at an impasse." She shrugged, a grin playing at her lips.

Curtis gave a heavy sigh, grinning as he did so. "So be it."

They strolled through the wrought iron gate that led them toward Mayfair. A few carriages passed before they crossed the cobbled street.

"I do have one request." He held his breath.

"Of course," she answered readily.

"Because I don't know who this gentleman is, and I trust you are not letting your family in on the secret…" He paused, watching for affirmation of his statement.

"Heavens, no." Her eyes grew wide with horror.

"…then please keep me updated on the events that transpire from this clandestine affair."

His arm stung with the sharp smack she delivered. "It is nothing of the sort!"

"Now." He eyed her meaningfully.

"Ever," she enunciated, "unless, well… unless he speaks with my parents, of course. But then it wouldn't be clandestine."

"Be that as it may, I just want to make sure you're safe." He paused in his stride and turned to her. "You've entrusted me with the secret. If you trust me with such a confidential matter, surely you can also trust my intentions in keeping you protected. All I ask is that when you hear from him, you simply tell me about it. Also, it adds the benefit that I might be able to deduce who your admirer is." He added a grin.

"Do you think?" she remarked with a heavy dose of enthusiasm.

Curtis engaged their walk once more. "One can never tell. I am quite good at uncovering secrets.

"Very well. But how do you propose we keep in contact? I cannot exactly write to you."

"That is a dilemma." He took a few steps and thought. "How about this? If we are to be at an event together sometime that week, then you'll save me a waltz, and we can speak. If there is no forthcoming event, then I'll simply stop by your residence, and we'll take a walk, just as we are doing now."

She nodded once. "That can work. However…" Her brow furrowed. "…if you are constantly waltzing with me and taking walks with me, won't people get the wrong idea? What if *he* gets the wrong idea?" She stopped suddenly, her eyes wide.

"My dear. I always waltz with you, and no talk has started. I'm also out walking with you, the second time this week, mind you, and I've heard no talk about it either. I'm quite the confirmed bachelor, you see. People know we have a friendship because of Lord and Lady Langley, so it's expected in a way. Plus, I'm not afraid of a little talk. Are you?" he challenged then held his breath.

"Of course not," Maria answered immediately.

"Then it's a plan." Curtis started walking once more, relieved that all was in place. But he slowed the pace, taking every opportunity to prolong the time with her.

"It's a plan. Will you be attending Lady March's rout tomorrow?"

"Will you be?" He turned the question.

"Yes. I have no other option. Mother responded in the affirmative weeks ago." Her tone was belabored.

"Don't curb your enthusiasm for my sake."

"I'll try." She offered a wan smile.

"Yes. I'll be there. And I'm so sure that you'll have news for me that I'll ask you to save me a waltz now and then."

"Done," she replied.

"Very good. And if I'm not mistaken, this is your residence, my lady."

"Indeed it is. Thank you, Mr. Sheppard." She released his arm and held out her hand.

He tempted fate by slowly taking it, kissing the gloved knuckles, and taking a selfish moment to inhale deeply, memorizing the scent before quickly releasing her hand and taking a step back from temptation.

She smiled kindly and turned to the stairs leading to her door. The maid — he had quite forgotten she was in tow —

followed quickly behind.

It wasn't like him to forget about any details.

It was concerning to think that he'd spent over an hour with Maria and not once remembered their chaperone. He'd have to be more vigilant in the future. If his plan was going to work, it had to be executed exactly.

With a firm nod, he made his way to his waiting carriage.

He had a letter to write.

# Chapter Six

A FEW HOURS after Maria's walk with Mr. Sheppard, a knock sounded at her door. Foolishly, she hoped it would be another letter, but she knew the chances of that occurrence were very slim. However, hope sprang eternal and without regard to probability.

The maid answered the door, and as Maxwell held out a silver tray, Maria's heart began to pound. It was only few moments, but it felt like a million as she watched the letter travel from the tray to the maid's hands and finally within her reach.

"Here, miss." Lottie dipped a quick curtsy and handed over the cream-colored envelope with the familiar wax seal.

"Thank you." The missive was thick, clearly holding more than one sheet of paper, and her heart tripped over the idea.

"Lottie, you are dismissed." She gave a hasty smile to her maid and willed her to leave quickly. When the door clicked shut, she withdrew her erasing knife and made short work of the now-familiar wax seal, the hint of sound like a million secrets spilling out.

Indeed, there was more than one sheet; rather, there were three, all neatly written. The anticipation of what they contained was almost too thick to bear, but she carefully sat at her desk and began to read.

> *Miss Garten*
>
> *I truly cannot express the joy I felt at seeing the lovely tulips in your window. I confess that I hoped against hope that you'd not find my communication unworthy, but to know that you're, perhaps skeptically, willing to converse with me is delightful.*
>
> *Surely, the first question you have is concerning my identity. After all, it would be the first question I'd ask if I were in your position. At risk of disappointing you, I'm going to immediately disclose that I'm not going to reveal my identity as of yet. Please, don't fret or be upset. I do feel it wise to give you a few particulars about my person to relieve some of your anxiety.*
>
> *I'm only just over my third decade in life, so you mustn't worry about some old codger trying to steal your vitality. No, I'm not currently attached to any other, so you can rest assured about my honorability. Yes, I am a gentleman, untitled but with more means than most titled, and a participant in the ton's inner circle. So, I'm not a footman or servant trying to win your heart — or money. I realize that this is quite frank and candid, but the truth often is. And I refuse to be anything but truthful. To be less is an insult to your character and mine.*

Maria bit back a grin. He was indeed candid. It was refreshing, delightful, and she appreciated that he deftly lay to rest most of the fears and questions she had.

Yet as much as he spoke about honestly, what if he wasn't? What if he were an exceptional liar? She mustn't be easy prey. With a decisive nod, she continued to read.

> *I've been given the privileged information of knowing you're planning to attend Lady March's rout tomorrow evening. May I please request a dance? I'm sure you'll be twirling all night; however, I'd love to have one moment with you in my arms, even if it's just for a minute… a second. Again, I'm continuing with the unknown identity, but just know that I'll be there…*
>
> *Honorably yours*

Maria rested the letter upon her desk, a small smile tipping her lips as she thought over the words just read. It was such a delightful and frightening mystery — and she wasn't certain which emotion won out. Regardless, she was already speculating about the rout tomorrow, curious as to who would be there.

And, more importantly, who would ask for a dance.

Taking a deep breath, she considered how many dances she usually partook of during a ball. She wasn't the most popular of debutants, nor was she a wallflower, so it shouldn't be too difficult to narrow down the gentlemen who could potentially be her admirer… once they asked for a dance, of course. Biting her lip, she reclined in her chair, a wide grin pulling her lip from its place between her teeth as she filled with nervous energy. It would be torture to wait till tomorrow night!

Of equal importance, what should she wear?

Standing promptly, she smoothed her skirts before she strode to her closet and scanned the colors. The palest of lavenders was the all the rage this Season, but in her mother's words, the color bled away her own.

And for once, she completely agreed with her.

The color was anything but complimentary, not to mention that everyone her age would be wearing a similar color.

And for once, she truly wanted to stand out.

Sweeping the dress aside, she scanned for another. As her eyes landed on a glimpse of stark white, she pulled the gown out farther, frowning as she tried to remember that particular one. Nodding, she recalled a late order she'd placed. It must have been delivered recently, and thus had never been worn. The bright white was so pure it almost had a blue cast. With a higher waistline, the dress's braided cord would tuck just under her breasts, accentuating them. She withdrew the dress then laid it on the bed and rang for Lottie.

In a few moments' time, Lottie knocked and entered upon Maria's invitation.

"How can I assist you, miss?" Lottie curtsied.

Maria gestured to the bed. "I need this dress prepared for tomorrow." "It might need airing and a hot iron."

"Of course, miss." Lottie quickly collected the garment with practiced movements and left to complete her mistress' request.

Maria nodded then found herself restless once more.

The dress was taken care of, but what now? That took up

only a few precious minutes, with what was she to distract herself?

She walked over to her nightstand and picked up a book. Taking a deep breath, she selected a chair beside the window and opened to her marked page.

Ten minutes later, Maria gave up. It was truly impossible to find any distraction! She set the book down, closed her eyes, and simply daydreamed. Why was this whole situation so delicious? It she were honest, it was because… she was wanted. It was a deliriously addictive feeling, one she hadn't ever experienced before. Oh, her parents loved her — tolerated her — but this was vastly different. A man, a young man of means and with an eloquent pen, found her worthy of perusal. It was even more fantastic because she didn't have to force the situation. It simply… was.

Her eyes opened wide as she considered a new thought. Perhaps she would finally get her first kiss! Her lips tickled at the thought, and instinctively she licked them. What would it be like? Would she *want* to kiss him? Would he want to kiss her? And what did she do when the opportunity presented itself? Dear Lord, how did one kiss?

What if she was terrible?

What if *he* was terrible at it?

There were so many variables! How did one navigate all this? She cast her gaze outside, trying to work through all the odd emotions. Yet, even as she sifted through them, she smiled. Though the expanse of feelings was frightening, she found that her joy remained the same, so did the anticipation for tomorrow. It grew even. Hope was a powerful thing; never had she fully understood its strength.

"Maria?" Her mother's voice preceded a sharp knock then a quick twist of her doorknob.

"Yes?" Maria stood quickly, smoothing her skirt out of habit.

"Dear, we have the Mayhews' card party tonight. Why are you not preparing for it?" Her mother's scolding tone stung slightly.

Maria felt a warm blush heat her face. How had she forgotten? "Forgive me, I'll make haste." She started toward her closet and stumbled slightly when she saw the letter.

Still lying on the desk, it was completely open, and if her mother were to simply walk a few steps, she could easily pick it up and read it.

Dear heavens!

How had she been so careless?

Maria thought quickly. "What would you suggest I wear?" she asked, her tone thin and anxious.

Lady Moray took a step toward her, dark brown eyebrows drawn together slightly as she regarded her daughter. "I'm sure your yellow gown will be lovely."

"Excellent." She swallowed, stepping intentionally in front of her desk, blocking her mother's view. With a desperate hope, she willed her mother to not be suspicious. "Would you mind ringing for Lottie?"

Lady Moray nodded once, turning to the bell, and as soon as her back was turned, Maria swept up the letter, folded it, and placed it under a book.

"Maria, I'll not read your diary. But if you think you're hiding something from me, you're quite mistaken."

Her mother's voice made Maria's gaze flick up. The cool sensation of dread was chased by relief at her mother's words. At least she thought it was private thoughts.

Which they were.

Just not… *her* private thoughts.

She bit back a grin.

"Thank you, Mother," she answered, trying to calm her racing heart.

As soon as her Lady Moray rang the bell, she turned. "I'll expect you ready in less than an hour. We wouldn't want them to wait for the final player, now would we?" Her mother's stern expression battled with Maria's efforts to calm her heart.

"Yes, ma'am." She nodded.

"Very well."

Without delay, her mother quit the room, and Maria almost fell into the chair as she legs weakened with relief that her secret was safe.

For now.

But she'd certainly learned an important lesson.

Letters would no longer be left out.

Even in her own room.

No. She needed a secret place to hide them.

And she knew just the place.

THE MAYHEWS' CARD party seemed to utterly drag on. As Maria tried to pay proper attention to the Whist cards before her, she found that her mind kept drifting away, thinking about all the possibilities tomorrow held.

"Did you hear that the Duchess Clairmont hasn't been seen for several weeks?" Lady Mayhew arched a brow as she glanced over her cards to her rapt audience.

"I had heard something similar, but I wasn't sure,"

another woman commented, casting a curious look between her cards and the hostess.

"Indeed," Lady Mayhew continued. "There's some talk about one of her wards missing!"

The air was filled with delicate gasps.

"You mean *missing* or simply… spending some time in the country?" Lady Spear gave a haughty glanced to her cards, her words thick with implication.

After all, young debutants didn't simply vanish unless they needed to. Many a ruined young lady had been sent to the country early in the Season, only to married hastily later.

Maria shifted in her seat at the uncomfortable twist in the conversation.

"I, for one, don't believe ill of any of the Lamont ladies." Maria's mother added to the conversation. "Well-bred, fine young women. Surely you don't mean to suggest that the duke's wards were trollops, Agnes?" Her mother's sharp regard pinned Lady Spear, who lowered her gaze.

"Of course. I'm simply relaying what I was told." She shrugged.

"Of course." Lady Moray played a card.

The room fell silent at Maria's mother's gentle scolding. But it wasn't long before Lady Mayhew added another bit of information.

"It's said that there's also some sort of mystery surrounding their family." She played a card with her usual fanfare and raised her chin as if reveling in the attention her gossip brought.

"Mystery, you say?" one of the ladies murmured. "Well, the duke has been known to be connected with Lord Langley. He was in the War Office, was he not?"

"Indeed," Lady Spear affirmed, giving Lady Moray an

arrogant glance.

"But surely he's retired..."

Lady Gleewood's nasal tone caused Maria to flinch slightly. How she wished she could simply leave!

"He's long since retired. If he weren't, how would we be even aware that he had connections with the War Office?" Lady Moray asked, her tone wry.

Lady Mayhew shrugged. "You have a point, dear. All in all, it is surely sad that any sort of ill will would be had toward the Duke and Duchess of Clairmont," she finished, playing her final hand and taking the last trick.

"Well, I do believe that ends it!" Lady Mayhew stood, a triumphant grin on her face, causing the crow's feet at her eyes to deepen.

"Congratulations." Maria's mother nodded kindly, even while she reached over and grasped her daughter's arm slightly, letting her know that they were to take their leave.

"I thank you for your invitation." Lady Spear stood, clutching her reticule as she gave a cold smile to Lady Mayhew, but it was to be expected. There was nothing warm or inviting about Lady Spear.

"Of course! I thank you for kindly attending my little gathering." Lady Mayhew simpered.

Maria wanted to roll her eyes at the false sincerity, but held her body in check.

"We will be on our way as well, Lady Mayhew. Thank you so much for extending the invitation to us." Lady Moray smiled warmly, but Maria could see the tight clench of her jaw. Though her mother loved gossip as much as the next lady, she wasn't one to simply enjoy the ill fate of others. Which was indeed what the ladies were glorifying in that evening.

"Thank you for attending." Lady Mayhew gave a slightly sincere smile toward Maria's mother, and with a short farewell to the other ladies, they found their way to the carriage waiting.

As the carriage lurched forward, Lady Moray released a deep breath. "At times I wonder why I accept her invitations."

"You did have true friends present," Maria reminded her, thinking on the almost-silent Lady Worrington, who was a stalwart friend of her mother's.

"Indeed, but even Elenora isn't worth attending if they are going to malign a family such as the Clairmonts. A duke, no less." She shook her head, causing her periwinkle hat to shake slightly.

"Jealousy," Maria answered.

"True. Still." Lady Moray twisted her lips. "Let us talk about more cheerful things. Have you selected your gown for Lady March's rout tomorrow eve?"

She almost asked if her father would attend, but she anticipated the answer. Lord Moray had rarely the time — rather the inclination — to attend such parties. In truth, he seldom had the tolerance for spending time outside his study at all.

Disregarding the thought, she turned her mind to more delightful musings. Maria felt a dreamlike anticipation fill her. With a determined breath, she collected herself before speaking. "Yes. I asked Lottie to press the white gown, the one with the blue hint? I do believe it will be lovely," Maria spoke, trying to calm her racing heart.

Her mother regarded her then nodded once. "I agree. It shall set you apart without bringing too much attention. A brilliant maneuver. You need all the help you can get."

Maria twisted her lips, her mother's words stinging.

Of course she would look at a ball as if requiring military strategy. Was she that hopeless in her mother's eyes? That they needed to be tactical in order to garner any gentlemen's attention? What a defeating thought!

Yet, it didn't sting nearly as much as usual. The whole idea was, as they say, water off a duck's back. It didn't stick, nor did it hurt… because she knew. There would be a gentleman waiting for her, her alone. He already was anticipating their meeting, and even if she wasn't aware of who he was, he was still there.

And for now, that was enough.

"Maria?" Her mother's voice called her back from her delightful musings.

"Yes?"

Lady Moray frowned slightly. "Is Mr. Sheppard going to be in attendance tomorrow?"

Maria blinked then thought back over their conversation. "I do believe he will be. Why?"

"Oh, no reason. Simple curiosity." Her mother smiled.

Maria narrowed her eyes.

Poor Curtis. Her mother already was making some sort of harebrained scheme. But how to distract her from setting her sights on him? After all, she had promised that she'd try to remove him from her mother's mental list of suitors.

"Lord Huffton walked me home the other day." She gave a shy grin to her mother, playing the part.

"Oh! He did, did he? He's quite eligible." She nodded approvingly. "I thought you were with Mr. Sheppard?"

"I was, but he forgot about an appointment and rather than rush me home, handed me over to Lord Huffton's care. He seemed very happy to accompany me," Maria added.

"Hmm…" The carriage hit a rut, rocking them slightly

as Maria watched her mother's expression shift to confusion, then understanding. "I see. Well, I would assume that if Mr. Sheppard had serious intentions, he'd not relinquish your care to another eligible gentleman. Odd, but Huffton is more of the catch, regardless. You could do worse, dear." Her mother's eyes twinkled.

Maria felt slightly ill. Not because of Lord Huffton, but because she was quite literally throwing him to the wolves.

And his only crime was having been kind enough to walk her home.

But it was either Lord Huffton or Mr. Sheppard, and the decision was an easy one.

"Indeed," Maria affirmed, wondering for the first time if maybe Lord Huffton sent the letters.

It was possible.

It was also probable.

Tomorrow would bless her with at least some answers.

After all, how many dances could an almost-spinster be asked to dance?

# Chapter Seven

**C**URTIS TOOK HIS time in preparing for the March rout. His evening kit was midnight-black in contrast with his starched white shirt. After debating between a gold or royal-blue cravat, he went with the blue.

Winston simply watched the silent mental debate.

"Not a word."

"Never, my lord." Winston cleared his throat and held out a hand to receive the length of silk.

Curtis lifted his chin slightly, watching in the mirror as Winston tied the difficult knot. When finished, his valet swept up the white gloves from the nearby desk and handed them to over. As Curtis tugged them into place, he mentally swore at their necessity.

Gloves.

Bloody useless.

Of course, that they would effectively prevent him from any sort of skin-on-skin-contact added to his dislike.

At the thought, his fingertips burned with the need to feel her skin, with the idea of its warmth and softness.

Worse, he realized that the truth was that it was all imagined. Never once had he touched Maria without gloves.

All the more reason to hate them.

"Sir?" Winston's voice drew him from his frustrations.

"Yes?" Curtis stood straight, tugging on the cuffs of his shirt.

"What pin?" Winston held up two cravat pins, both of which were quite similar; only the practiced eye would see the difference.

"The smaller." Curtis jerked his chin to the left and waited as Winston fastened the small gold-and-ruby-inlayed pin to his cravat before holding up his evening coat. The fit was snug but would allow for enough movement to waltz. And just like that, his attention was focused on the events forthcoming.

Tonight, he'd waltz with Maria.

But unlike all the other times he'd danced with her, this would be the first time he was also pursuing her. Odd how it changed everything. Of course, that she was unaware he was pursuing her added to the anticipation, but the truth remained.

With any luck, someday she'd be his.

His body ached with the deep need for it, but tonight he had to play two roles.

And he needed to be clear-minded, clear-headed.

Or else he could ruin it all.

So, as he left his residence and entered his carriage, he forced a calm he didn't feel, breathing slowly through his nose and focusing on the clip-clop of the matched bays hooves on the London cobble. In a few minutes, he arrived at the March residence in Mayfair and waited as the carriage paused in queue. After the carriages deposited their patrons before the entrance, each rolled on, making room for another. He studied the carriages before him, noticing that none of them bore the crest of Lord and Lady Moray; however, one crest caught his eye.

The Duke of Clairmont's coach was rolling forward, just ahead of his own conveyance. As it trundled to the front entrance, Curtis slid over to the other window to get a better view. Sure enough, the duke and duchess alighted from the carriage and toward the foyer. They had been somewhat reclusive as of recent. The evening had just proven far more interesting than he had anticipated. The case he was investigating was the disappearance of the duke's ward, Miss Beatrix Lamont. As of yet, he hadn't spoken with the duke; tonight would prove an excellent opportunity to at least make an appointment.

Perhaps after a waltz.

Or two.

And most certainly, after he earned a smile from Maria and had a chance to kiss her gloved hand— He silently cursed the gloves all over again.

As his carriage rolled to the entrance, Curtis stepped down and made a mental note of where the duke and duchess waited to be announced. Giving a quick nod to a footman, he passed by several conversing couples and strode to the entryway of the stately white stone townhome. Torches lined the cobbled path to the door, their slight smoke a welcome fragrance to the normally pungent air of London. As a slight rain fell, it sizzled on the burning wicks. As he approached, the duke and duchess were just being announced, and he cursed his missed opportunity. Though it would be much better to speak with him sequestered, a crowded room proved often more private than most would imagine.

"Mr. Curtis Sheppard," he murmured to the servant announcing arrivals, and, without waiting for his name, he entered, scanning the various member of the *ton* all laughing and conversing, creating a dull roar in the wide foyer. He quickly ascended the stairs that would lead to the second-floor ballroom then paused at the entrance, looking over the now-swirling couples as they all danced. He caught sight of the duke and duchess and strode toward them, purposefully ignoring the primal need to search for Maria. If he saw her now, she'd completely distract him from his need to speak with the duke. And he must seize the opportunity as it presented itself.

As he approached the Duke of Clairmont, the man turned as if anticipating his arrival. "Sheppard." He arched a dark brow over his unreadable blue eyes.

*Ah, so he was already aware.*

"Your grace." Curtis nodded, giving a smile to the blonde beauty beside the duke.

"May I present my wife, the Duchess of Clairmont."

Curtis bowed respectfully before turning his attention back to the duke. "If I could have a moment?"

"Indeed. Is it a venue of conversation that should wait for the privacy of my office?"

"Yes. Would it be acceptable for me to call tomorrow around four?" Curtis asked, a curiosity tickling his spine. He wasn't able to pinpoint it, but something seemed… off.

"That would be acceptable. Now if you'll excuse us?" The duke gave a quick smile and walked away in an overly relaxed manner.

Curtis watched, the feeling as if he were missing a vital puzzle piece growing stronger. Clairmont was highly attached to his wards, that was common knowledge. Yet one was missing…

He didn't appear affected.

Even by the implication that Curtis had information about his missing ward.

The mystery ate away, distracting him fully till a soft, lilting voice jolted him back to the present.

"I've always loved a gentleman in a black coat." Maria flirted.

He turned, his heart slamming against his chest at her words. While he knew they were on friendly enough terms for her to joke with him, it affected him differently. For her to say such a thing meant that she did find him attractive.

Damn it all, he was reading into everything like a woman.

"And I do love a debutant in a…" Curtis paused, taking in her gown, drinking her in. "Good Lord, Maria," he murmured hoarsely, swallowing hard and immediately berating himself for being so careless with his words. He cleared his throat and forced a charming grin. "You're lovely! Quite angelic, if I say so myself… even if I know better."

"Thank you, I think." She grinned wryly. Her gaze shifted to the room, scanning it thoughtfully.

"Looking for someone?" Curits asked, deftly angling toward her, moving in closer.

"Yes. You know I am, thank you kindly," she answered, not even turning slightly to address his question.

"Have you had any more… contact?" he asked, knowing full well she had.

"Maybe, maybe not." She shrugged.

"Oh, is that how you're going to play it, minx? Confide in me and then leave me out in the dark?" he joked, using her distraction as the prime opportunity to scan her features, catalogue them in that devastatingly beautiful gown. His mouth grew dry as he noted the way the braided cord accentuated the swell of her perfect breasts, while draping with the barest of hints over her round derriere. Dear Lord, she was killing him without a weapon.

"Very well, you have a point. It's not very sporting of me to keep you in the dark when you've been nothing but supportive." Maria gave a small sigh. "He said that I'll dance with him tonight." She turned, her gaze alive with delight, practically overwhelming him with a humbling elation.

She was this excited about him… only she didn't know it was *him*.

Would she be so thrilled if she knew?

The thought was sobering, and he cleared his throat before responding. "Ah, so some of the mystery will be solved then!"

"Yes! Of course, no one has asked me to dance yet, but… maybe he hasn't arrived." She gave him a slightly worried look, her dark-winged brows drawing together slightly.

"Well, just because he's not made his move doesn't mean you have to be a wallflower. Let's take the next dance and give him something to be jealous over, don't you think?" He leaned in closely, inhaling softly the scent of rosewater clinging to her shoulder as he paused just above it.

She sighed and turned then paused. Her green eyes wide, she blinked at his proximity before blushing as he gave her a wink and offered his hand.

"You're wounding my ego," he said as he wiggled his still-empty hand, his heart pounding hard at the thought of her rejection.

"Sorry, yes, of c-course." She seemed to collect herself and placed her hand in his.

How could holding a woman's hand be so sensual? Yet, as his grip tightened slightly over hers, his body responded. He forced his thoughts away from the path they tried to take, one that led to visions of that very same dress pooled in a heap on his bedroom floor. "How are the tulips?" he asked, forcing his thoughts into line.

"Alive. How chivalrous of you to care." She arched a brow at him, grinning.

"That's me. What can I say? I care about children, small animals, and tulips. I'm a regular saint." He chuckled as they meandered through the room toward the dancing floor.

Maria stifled a giggle.

"Mocking me?" Curtis asked.

"Never." Her eyes were a mask of innocence, an expression that at once had him narrowing his eyes.

"And a lady such as yourself would never stoop to use sarcasm," he answered with a hint of sarcasm and a grin.

"Indeed. Never," she replied haughtily then proceeded to giggle. "Never!" she repeated with exaggeration.

Curtis chuckled, taking pleasure in the way her grin lit up her countenance, enchanting him. Yet as his gaze left her face, he noticed the regard of several other gentlemen as well, watching her thoughtfully.

With interest.

Bloody hell.

"Shall we?" He led her out to the floor to the beginning of the quadrille. As they performed the steps and spun around, he grinned at the way she danced with graceful abandon. While her steps were perfectly executed, a lively nature reflected the wit and humor she possessed. How had he missed that before? As she gave him playful grins, he found himself lost in the merriment of the moment. Was this what he had been afraid to face? Had he truly felt that a life of lonely bachelorhood could compare to this carefree joy?

The song ended all too soon, and before they exited the floor, Lord Huffton approached, asking Maria for a dance. She obliged, and as they turned to the dance floor, she glanced back, giving Curtis a wide-eyed grin full of implication.

Damn it all, for the rest of the night she'd think each partner could potentially be her admirer. She'd laugh, flirt, and beam those beautiful smiles in their direction.

While he watched.

And bloody hell, he had no one to blame for it but himself.

# Chapter Eight

CURTIS ARRIVED AT home in a foul mood. He had tried to snag a final dance with Maria, but it seemed that the more gentlemen danced with her, the more in demand she had become. Had she even waited out one dance? He thought not. While strategically, it was helpful that there were so many contributors to his anonymity, it was also bloody horrible to see her in that many other men's arms. What had caused such a ripple effect? It was as if every gentleman suddenly realized the rare treasure and wanted it for himself. But they were too little, too late.

Because he wasn't about to give up.

The only arms that should be holding her were his.

Ever.

Damn it all, he needed to step up his game. What had begun as a slow and methodical plan now needed to accelerate like a racing curricle. But how?

It wasn't as if he could simply tell her the truth.

No, that would be too easy, and he needed to know first…

Know if she wanted him. But what if she didn't? His mood darkened further, to the point that he almost missed the light tap on his bedroom door. With a muffled curse, he bade them enter. Winston arched a brow as he walked through the door holding out a missive, and Curtis paused. He reached out and took the envelope from his butler then dismissed him. Sliding his finger through the top to loosen the wax seal, his heart pounded as he recognized the imprint.

Neville.

After tearing the envelope open, he quickly read the letter. It would seem that the missing heiress had been found, but not in the manner they had assumed. The War Office was under the impression that she had been kidnapped.

Neville's information stated that she was with a family friend.

Odd.

Not only that, but that he was betrothed to the heiress!

Curtis blinked, reading the sentence again. Neville? Engaged? On purpose? The world must have turned on its ear!

Taking a fortifying breath, he continued to read. Neville requested that he find out an update on where they stood as to locating the source of the trouble with the Lamont family. He didn't feel at ease bringing his betrothed to London when they knew so little about the threat.

The rational side of Curtis thought that was rather understandable, but the other areas of his brain were trying to process the idea that Neville was betrothed.

Neville. The man that had every right, every intention in the world to stay unattached was now intentionally betrothed. It went against everything he knew about him!

Just as he was reading the final instructions, another knock sounded.

"Well, aren't I the popular one tonight?" he grumbled,

striding to the door and swinging it wide.

Winston rewarded him with a wry grin. "Pardon, but there is one more missive, my lord."

On alert, Curtis slowly took it from his butler's hand, narrowing his eyes as he studied the man. "Is it…" he asked, letting the words linger.

"Yes."

"Summon Henry. I've learned some new information, and I'm going to be needing his assistance."

"At once, my lord." With a quick bow, the butler left, closing the door softly behind him.

Curtis studied the unmarked envelope, knowing its unidentifiable markings meant one thing.

It was from the War Office.

"Bloody hell, what's happened now?" he muttered as he tore into the envelope.

Sure enough, the letter bore the official seal and was dated just that evening.

> *Mr. Sheppard,*
>
> *We have uncovered some information about the Lamont Case. It would seem that a Sir Richard Kirby has passed through several local magistrates with a case seeming to prove his familial relation with the Lamont family — and his rightful inheritance of their estate via familial marital contract. At this point, we are unable to discern the validity of his claims.*
>
> *We've also received news that Sir Kirby has sent men into the countryside trying to locate Miss Beatrix Lamont, as she is the oldest sister who is unattached. Because of the delicate nature*

*of the threat, we cannot ascertain if Sir Kirby is the origin, or if this is simply a coincidence. In the meantime, please take precaution.*

*If you learn any news of Neville, Miss Lamont or Sir Kirby, please inform us directly through the usual means.*

*Regards,*
*Officer Reynolds, Esq.*

"Damn and blast." Curtis swore under his breath. He paced the wood floors, his boots clicking as he strode back and forth in front of the fire. On the positive side, Miss Beatrix Lamont had been found and was with a family friend. So, they could be assured that this Sir Kirby fellow hadn't located her. Yet.

On the more harrowing side, Sir Kirby was pursuing a legal attachment to the Lamont family, particularly Beatrix Lamont — Neville's intended. It was a blasted Greek tragedy!

Yet, as he considered the claims that Sir Kirby was trying to prove, it didn't add up. Years ago, the Lamont sisters were given as wards to the Duke of Clairmont — a shirttail relation if there ever was one! In fact, the duke was the only relation they had been able to tie the girls to when a carriage accident claimed the life of their parents. And even that attachment to the duke was a precarious one. So, if the only relation they could find as guardian for the girls was one that was a stretch, how was it that Sir Kirby was able to claim such a close relation now? It didn't add up.

Which was probably why he was pursuing Miss Beatrix Lamont. If he could marry her, convincing her solely on his word, then he would not have to prove anything.

Curtis shook his head. That simply had to be the answer. But regardless, he needed to gather information on the bloke.

He also had to notify Neville.

His night had gone from hell to hellfire.

Mumbling an oath, he strode to the door and called for Winston.

As he took the stairs down toward his study, Winston approached from the hall, Henry in tow.

"Perfect. At least something this evening is going right." Curtis clipped the words as he nodded a greeting to the young man.

"Sir?" Winston raised his eyebrows.

"Yes, Winston. I need you to make arrangements for my early departure in the morning. I'll be gone no longer than a few days, but it will need to be… discreet."

"Of course. When will you wish to depart?" he asked.

"Five a.m. No later. And please ask Cook to pack enough provisions for me to break my fast and supply the noon meal." A grin tugged at his lips. Cook would no doubt see to it that he had enough food to feed an entire English regiment.

"Right away, my lord." Winston bowed and silently left, taking a right toward the kitchens.

"Leaving, eh?" Henry asked, striding toward Curtis' study.

"Yes." Curtis sighed the word. "I assume you know something of why I summoned you here?"

"I'm piecing things together." Henry shrugged. His black great coat stretched across overly broad shoulders for his barely adult body. But even at the young age of ten and eight, he had been a force to be reckoned with. Having grown up on the rougher side of London, he was a fierce fighter and able to blend into any situation.

A skill they would need.

"What do you know of Sir Richard Kirby?" Curtis asked as he gestured to a chair for Henry and proceeded to close his study door.

Henry sat, leaning forward on his knees. His dark brows furrowed. "Kirby, eh? He's new to town. A few men have talked about him at White's… but nothing of note. Why?"

Curtis walked to the sideboard, poured himself a glass of port, and sipped. "He's currently in town with the hope of proving his connection to the Lamont family — and establishing a marital contract with Miss Beatrix Lamont. He claims he is a close-enough relation to be entitled to their sizable estate."

"Bollocks," Henry scoffed. "A lie if I've ever heard one. Wasn't the duke barely connected with the family?"

"Indeed."

"Then how is Sir Kirby able to prove anything?" Henry asked, shrugging slightly and relaxing into the brocaded chair.

"He can't. But… for him to pass through the local magistrates means that he's either a good liar, or he's who he says he is."

"He's a good liar," Henry answered immediately.

"I'm with you. But we have to prove that."

"So, you want me to tail him?" Henry sat up, anticipation gleaming his expression.

"Yes. I'm departing tomorrow to locate Neville." Curtis poured another glass of port and extended it to Henry.

"He's found her then?" Henry asked, taking a sip of the amber liquid.

"Apparently, and took it a step further and spoke for her."

Henry coughed, sputtering on his sip of port as his eyes

narrowed at Curtis. "Say what?"

"He's betrothed, to Beatrix Lamont."

Henry cleared his throat. "You're certain?"

"He told me in a missive just this evening."

"On purpose?" Henry asked the next obvious question for those who were familiar with Neville's history.

"Apparently."

"Bloody hell. It must have completely frozen over."

"My sentiments exactly." Curtis raised his glass.

Henry swirled the port in his glass. "That thickens the soup, doesn't it?"

"Just a bit."

Curtis took a long swallow, letting the port burn down his throat and settle, warm in his stomach.

"Does he know?" Henry asked, taking a cautious sip.

"No. Neville isn't aware of Kirby, or his intentions."

Henry whistled lowly.

"You see why I'm departing tomorrow?" Curtis gave an unamused grin.

"I wouldn't want to be in your boots when you tell him."

"I don't want to be in my boots either," Curtis answered honestly. Neville would go wild.

Henry took another sip and then stood. "If that's all, then I'd best be going and see if I can find our target." He set the glass on the table beside the chair and nodded, turning toward the door.

"Henry, I'll return in two days' time. Please have some information to report. I'll likely have Neville with me, and I expect he'll be like a caged tiger."

"Lovely," Henry replied with dry sarcasm and left.

Immediately, Curtis wrote and dispatched a missive to the Duke of Clairmont, giving his apologies for being unable to meet him at the appointed time, stating that business had called him away. Knowing that the Duke's ward, Miss Beatrix Lamont, was not actually missing but with a family friend clarified the duke's puzzling reactions from earlier. It didn't sit well, though. Why would he send her away then pretend she was missing? To protect her?

Curtis sipped his port and finished the rest, watching as the fire licked the wood in the study fireplace.

As he set the glass down on the wood table, he noticed a book open on his desk, the bright colors in the page drawing his eye.

He frowned for a moment as the realization hit him, and he groaned.

Maria.

Of all the horrific times to have to leave London.

After the ball.

When dozens of gentlemen were now likely to call on her, he wouldn't be in their ranks.

He'd be in the bloody countryside.

He had to make some sort of move, but what? And how could he at this hour?

Good Lord, there wasn't enough port in the world to deal with tonight's problems!

He turned back to the fire, studying its flames, hoping for inspiration to hit him.

Finally, a smile curled his lips as he thought of a perfect plan. It would be a risk — but nothing ventured, nothing gained.

And he certainly hoped he'd be gaining something.

Gaining someone.

Maria.

# Chapter Nine

"WHAT IN HEAVEN'S name is all this?" Lady Moray slowly descended the stairs with an expression of confusion and delight.

Maria bit her lip, trying to keep her smile to one that wasn't overly large, when all she wanted to do was sing, dance, and smile so wide her face would hurt for days!

Flowers had started to arrive at eight a.m. sharp, an ungodly hour for those amongst the *ton* who had spent the night dancing away, but it was a welcomed delight for Maria!

Even if she hadn't woken till near noonday!

Every shade of tulip created a kaleidoscope of color that fairly overwhelmed the hall as the servants were hard-pressed to find enough vases to hold them all. On the hour, more flowers would arrive, and none of them held any note.

But Maria knew who'd sent them.

Well, not exactly, but close enough.

For now.

"Well, I'd say that the March's rout was a smashing success, based on the amount of floral décor we have this morning." Her mother touched a red tulip and grinned at her daughter.

"Possibly." Maria couldn't help her smile this time, allowing it to spread wide across her face.

"Who are they from?" Lady Moray asked one of the parlor maids.

"I'm not sure, my lady. There've been no notes attached. And when Maxwell asks about the sender, the deliverer says that they haven't a clue either."

"Well, another mystery..." Lady Moray eyed Maria, studying her as if trying to unlock the secret.

"I'm just as shocked as you, Mother." Maria forced an innocent expression, hoping it wasn't too much.

"Well, they truly are lovely, even if we're nearly swimming in them. This can't help but add to your desirability." Her mother's eyes gleamed as she took in the sight.

"Pardon?" Maria frowned.

"Dear! Later, when we receive callers, they will walk through this almost-vulgar display of flowers and know that they are not the only ones interested in you." Her mother gave a dainty shrug. "And men love a little healthy competition."

"Oh. Well, that's good?" Maria tried to sound relieved. But truthfully, she was only interested in one pursuit.

If she only knew who he was.

"Come Maria! We only have a few hours to prepare for callers. I'm thinking you'll be lovely in your lavender day gown, and I'll have my lady's maid coif your hair. We want this to be perfect. We might only have one shot." She turned back and gave her daughter a meaningful look.

Maria felt her shoulders cave in slightly, knowing full well what that expression meant.

Be quiet.

Don't laugh too loudly.

Short sentences.

Be ladylike.

Don't be yourself.

And more than anything, she wished she just knew who her admirer was… because all those things that her mother hated? He had mentioned that he liked.

And it was quite wonderful to be appreciated for who she was… not who other people wanted her to be.

"Maria?" her mother clipped.

Shaking her head, Maria forced a smile and followed Lady Moray. Casting a last longing glaze to the tulips, she exhaled a sigh and took the stairs.

Even though she had several hours before gentlemen would be calling, her mother demanded she start preparing. So, after being fluffed, coiffed, corseted to the point of fainting, and dressed, she had more than an hour to wait. Even if corsets weren't in vogue, her mother was quite determined that her figure would be finer than was natural. Being properly attired, according to her mother's standards, and early as well, she had nothing to do but wait.

Because she couldn't go below stairs. What if gentlemen arrive early and she was there waiting? That wouldn't be good at all! Or so her mother said.

Nor could she be walking around, because then she would surely faint from lack of oxygen — her own musings.

As she shifted, trying to adjust one of the bones in the corset that was particularly nasty, she wondered if maybe her mother had her cinched so tight in efforts to keep her from being able to speak much.

It seemed perfectly plausible.

*Drat.*

So, unable to move or breathe well, Maria shifted from her reclining chair to gaze out the window.

A knock startled her, but once she regained some of her lost and miserably tight breath, she bade them enter.

"A letter, miss, from Miss Rebecca Lockett. Also, another from Lady Langley." Lottie extended the parchment envelopes to her mistress, and Maria accepted them with a smile.

"Thank you, Lottie. That will be all."

With a quick curtsy, Lottie left, closing the door gently.

Maria tore into the letter from Rebecca, unwilling to walk to the desk for her erasing knife, or wait to attain it.

A warm smile tugged at her lips as she read the familiar handwriting.

> *Miss Garten,*
>
> *I must say, you are looking particular fetching today. Your eyes sparkle like the ocean at sunset, and each time I'm with you, you utterly steal my breath with your wit and beauty.*
>
> *All these are words I wish to speak to you in person — but alas, I cannot. I've been called away from London for several days, and while my heart is with you, I cannot be there with it. Please enjoy the lovely tulips, one for each moment I'll be thinking of you while I'm away.*
>
> *And when I return, I do hope to make a more familiar acquaintance with you, if you're willing.*
>
> *Sincerely yours*
>
> *P.S. It was my sincere and utter delight to dance with you last night. As always, you're*

> *a brilliant partner, and I've always enjoyed dancing with you…*

Maria re-read the letter, committing it to memory as she bit her lip and grinned. Yet as she finished, her heart pinched with the knowledge that she wouldn't see her admirer today. And she'd rather anticipated that she would. When she considered the circumstance, it really was quite wonderful! She could easily write off every other gentleman that called on her from the list of possible admirers! Assuming that any gentlemen did arrive to call on her.

It was quite thoughtful of him, to notify her that he'd be out of town. She rather appreciated his consideration. So often it seemed like men of the *ton* did whatever they wished with little consideration to their wives. She hoped that this might mean that her admirer was different.

She could hope, couldn't she?

As she set the letter on her lap, she picked up the second. She studied the letter with curiosity. Why would Lady Olivia Langley be sending her a missive? With a shrug that reminded her how tight her corset was, she slipped a finger through the envelope and opened the letter.

A short message was scrawled across the page.

> *"Maria, this is an odd request, but would you please keep your ears open for gossip regarding a Sir Richard Kirby? I'd be most grateful. I'll speak with you in a few days.*
>
> *Curtis*

"Odd." Maria turned over the single sheet of paper, re-

read it, then grinned. Leave it to Curtis to find a way to contact her without alerting her mother. Poor man, as it was, Maria was still trying to steer her mother away from the idea of his eligibility.

She glanced at the letter, memorizing the name. *Sir Richard Kirby*. It wasn't familiar, but that didn't necessarily signify anything of importance. London was quite vastly populated with people of the *ton* shifting in and out at their own discretion. She thought it rather odd that he'd ask her to be aware, but it was the least she could do after all he'd done for her.

Even if she didn't need the list anymore.

He still had braved her mother and befriended her.

So she set them all aside. As she started to put each back in the proper envelope, she gasped.

Narrowing her eyes, she picked up the letters and held them side by side. There was a strange similarity, but not enough to discern if they'd been written by the same person, but the envelopes…

As she set down the letters and picked up the envelopes, her heart started to pound.

*Miss Rebecca Lockett*
*Lady Langley*

The L's were exactly the same. In fact, every aspect of the handwriting was identical.

She glanced back to the letters, holding them up closer to her face.

No. They were different. Not much… but enough that she couldn't be certain.

But that didn't mean she didn't *suspect*.

No.

Curtis?

Her mind spun! Never had she actually considered…

No, she had. Many times. But she'd stopped those thoughts in their tracks, never imagining that he'd consider her.

Never imagining that he'd consider *anyone,* at least seriously.

But what if?

Well, that changed everything.

But how could she tell?

It was a quandary! Because, while she suspected, there was no way she was going to risk his friendship by asking him outright. How humiliating should she be wrong!

But, as she lifted the envelopes again, there was a real chance she might be right as well.

She sat back, closing her eyes and thinking about the letters. Were there clues?

The most obvious was that her admirer was going out of town… and Curtis had said he would see her in a few days. Did that mean he was out of town as well? Then it could be easily assumed that they were one and the same?

Dear Lord, her head was spinning!

And as she thought, she paused. What if… What if it was Curtis?

Did she want it to be him?

Why would he go to all the trouble of remaining anonymous?

It didn't make any sense.

She tried to breathe deep but cursed under her breath when her attempt was foiled.

Blasted corset and her mother's old-fashioned notions!

"Maria! It's almost time. Are you ready, dear?" Her mother knocked, speaking loudly, earning Maria's glare toward the door.

She quickly slid the letters under a cushion, just in case.

"One moment." Maria tried to sound sweet, but it came out as more of a groan. Not only could she not breathe, but she wouldn't see her admirer, and, of all things, the one man she considered a friend might actually be a whole lot more.

Life was utterly complicated at the moment.

"Maria!" Her mother called in a sharp tone.

With a pathetically defeated sigh, she rose and stiffly walked to the door, forcing a smile as she faced her mother.

Hell had no fury like a matchmaking mama.

"You look ill," her mother commented, studying her face.

It was probably the weak attempt at a smile, Maria suspected, but she shook her head. "I'm quite well. Shall we?" She strode down the hall and toward the stairs, slowing her pace considerably as she took the steps, not wanting to be winded by reaching the final one.

Her mother's footsteps sounded behind her, and as she landed on the lower floor, she waited for Maxwell, who was showing a gentleman into the parlor to the right.

When he turned back and spotted Maria, he bowed his head.

"Maxwell," her mother called from behind her, "who are we receiving?"

Maxwell extended his silver tray to Lady Moray, and she quickly flipped through the crisp cards, reading each name silently. "Splendid." She set them back on the tray and walked ahead of Maria. "Shall we?"

Maria nodded, and followed her mother into the blue

parlor, taking mental notes.

Lord Washburn.

Sir Crackston

Lord Treyson

Lord Huffton.

She nodded to each gentleman in turn as he rose, each offering a polite and interested smile.

It was everything she had always hoped.

And it all fell flat. Because she knew… he wasn't in the room.

But that didn't mean she couldn't give these gentlemen a kind smile and a moment of her time. After all, she was a lady.

But none of them would ever have her heart.

It was a wonderful and clarifying moment.

And as the afternoon progressed, she checked off several other names.

She bided her time and was finally able to excuse herself after dinner, complete with her mother's incessant gushing over her daughter's smashing popularity. With a breath held tight, Lottie finally removed her wretched corset, and at last, she was able dismiss her maid and pull out the list.

The. List.

And as she withdrew it from her desk, she slowly checked off all but two names.

Mentally, she added a third.

Mr. Curtis Sheppard.

Three gentlemen.

As she studied the list once again, she tried to remember if she had danced with either of the remaining men at the March's rout.

She rather thought that she had, but the evening had

been quite the swirl of activity.

So, no definitive evidence for or against her suspicions of Curtis.

It was beyond complicated and confusing.

As she set the list down on her desk, she breathed out a sigh…

Then sat up straight.

*Wait.*

She quickly slid open her drawer with the other letters from her admirer and placed them out before her. Next, she laid the list that Curtis had written and compared them all.

Her gaze darted from each sheet of parchment.

Studying every line, each flick of the pen.

With a dainty hand raised to her mouth, she leaned back in her chair, closing her eyes.

Her secret admirer wasn't so secret after all.

# Chapter Ten

CURTIS RODE THROUGH the English countryside in his new carriage, making excellent time as he crested the hill toward Breckridge House, the country residence of the notorious Lady Southridge.

He shuddered at the name.

There were stories. And he believed them all.

Thankfully, the stories were of her matchmaking prowess, and apparently, her legend was continuing. Neville had become betrothed under her watch.

She also happened to be the one who was hiding Beatrix Lamont.

It was an odd connection, but a well-known one for its ferocity. Lady Southridge was much older than her brother, who was best chums with the Duke of Clairmont. When the duke's parents had met an early grave, she'd moved in and never stepped out of the role as parent. So, while she wasn't actually related, no one dared question her loyalty to the duke and his family, including his wards. If rumors were true, she loved the wards even more than the duke.

Of course, one couldn't always believe the rumors.

But he rather leaned toward believing this one.

Large black gates were wide open as his driver slowed the carriage down as they approached the entrance to the estate. When the carriage finally stopped, Curtis immediately hopped out and proceeded to knock on the door.

"Yes?" An elderly butler studied him with a sharp eye, reminiscent of an old owl.

"I'm here to see Lady Southridge." Curtis extended his card, hoping to simply gain an audience without having to give away how much he knew. It wasn't likely that there were spies in the house, but he didn't want to risk Neville's or Beatrix's identity.

"One moment." The butler studied the card and closed the door, almost smashing Curtis' boot in the process.

Curtis glared at the door and frowned. Waiting. He hated it.

Not long later, the door opened to a vibrant, redheaded dowager who studied him from head to toe, her gaze sharp and alert.

"Mr. Sheppard." She spoke his name sharply.

"Yes. You must be Lady Southridge." He bowed crisply.

"Indeed. What took you so long, young man?" She turned and walked into the house, glancing behind her. "Hurry up. We haven't all day."

Curtis blinked and followed her into the foyer then to the right as a footman opened the door to a green parlor.

"Neville isn't here. He left this morning to check on the post — expecting a letter from you." She gave him an accusing glance as she took a seat then motioned for him to take one as well.

"Yes, well, this is news better delivered in person, as I'm sure he will have multiple questions regarding it."

"What news?" She leaned forward.

"I'm afraid I cannot disclose such sensitive information—"

"Bloody hell, you can. And Neville isn't setting foot into this room till you spill why you came from London personally. And don't doubt my word." She tilted her chin.

"Forgive me, my lady, but I will—"

"Mr. Sheppard. If I were a threat to… Bev…" She let the words linger in the air, watching him meaningfully. "…then her guardian wouldn't have sent me away with her, would he?"

Curtis narrowed his eyes. Beatrix was not a Bev… so that meant that she was still undercover. This was good. Sir Kirby would have extreme difficulty in finding her because of the different name. It was brilliant.

"Well done," he conceded.

"So you'll tell me?" She smiled.

"No."

"You're a difficult one, aren't you?" She twisted her lips. "Very well. I'll go first. But we will need tea. This is a long story. And in the meantime, I'll send a footman out toward town, hoping to intercept Neville. He's probably taking his bloody time since he's with… Bev." She rolled her eyes and rang for tea.

And a long story it was indeed.

The duke had sent Beatrix away with Lady Southridge, hoping to create a ruse that she was missing. Threats had been issued toward the Lamont sisters because of the size of their inherited estate. When they couldn't find the source of the intimidations, the duke had taken matters into his own hands, and Lady Southridge had spirited her away to Breckridge house.

Where she remained under the guise of a lady's maid named Bev. Neville had somehow found the needle in the haystack and suspected Lady Southridge of harboring her… and one thing had then led to another.

"But I still don't understand how they are betrothed," Curtis said. He glanced at his tea where it sat growing cold.

"Another long story… "

Curtis groaned.

"Men. I'll shorten it for you. He loves her." After a wave of her hand, she picked up her teacup and took a dainty sip.

Curtis waited, but she shrugged and set her teacup down, folding her hands demurely.

"That's all?"

"Does there need to be more?" she asked.

"Often times, yes," Curtis answered, his patience wearing thin.

"They knew each other from before, if that helps. Being here simply… accelerated the process. Honestly, he hasn't had eyes for anyone since that horrible mess with his wife. Good mercy." She sighed emphatically.

"Ah, so you know about that, eh?" Curtis tugged at his shirtsleeves, feeling exceedingly uncomfortable with the conversation.

"Young man, I know more than you can imagine." She gave a wink. "Your turn. I told my side."

He took a breath. Honesty, with what she had disclosed, there was no reason to keep her in the dark, or at least not to tell her some of it. "Very well. What we know is that whatever threat toward the Lamont sisters isn't as prominent as before, but there is a new issue. Do you know of a Sir Richard Kirby?"

"Kirby? No. Why?" Her green eyes sharpened.

"He's claiming to have a connection to the Lamont estate, and he's hoping to seal it by marrying the most eligible sister." He let the words sink in.

"Beatrix."

"Yes."

"Well, that simply won't do. And Neville is going to have a fit at the thought," she scoffed, shivering delicately.

"But there is one hitch. He claims that he has a right to marry one of the sisters and gain the estate. Sisters. Beatrix and Roberta are the only ones unmarried."

"And Beatrix wouldn't allow some stranger — a charlatan at best — to try and arrange a marriage contract with her little sister."

"She'd do it herself before that," Curtis finished.

"Damn it all."

Curtis coughed, shocked at hearing Lady Southridge's low words.

"Your delicate ears offended?" she joked, and then she sobered. "What are we to do?"

"Well, it would seem that Kirby is actively looking for Beatrix." Curtis stood up and began pacing.

Lady Southridge opened her mouth, but a stirring in the foyer had her closing it and rising from her chair.

In short order, Lord Neville and a young lady, Curtis could only assume was Miss Beatrix Lamont, burst into the room.

"Neville." Curtis nodded once, taking in the man before him. He was a dangerous one, though few knew it. Loyal to a fault, but lethal.

"Curtis…" Neville replied, turning to Beatrix. "…allow me to introduce Bev—"

"Hang it all, Neville. Everyone already knows. Just call her Beatrix." Lady Southridge's irritated tone broke through his introduction.

His gaze cut to her then to Curtis. "Is that so?" His expression was dark as his brows drew together over his gray eyes.

"Indeed. Which is why I decided to visit rather than converse by post. We have quite the… dilemma. But if you'll please finish introductions," Curtis requested in a calm voice, trying to alleviate the fear growing in her expression.

"Apologies. This is Miss Beatrix Lamont. Miss Lamont, may I introduce you to Mr. Curtis Sheppard."

"A pleasure." Beatrix smiled, but it was forced.

"The delight is all mine. As a gentleman, one can never tire of making the acquaintance of such a beautiful lady." Curtis spoke in his most flirtatious manner, hoping to dissipate some of the tension in the room. It seemed to work.

"*My* lady," Neville replied tersely, his tone more than a little possessive.

"Is that so?" Curtis asked in a goading tone. "Then that either complicates matters or solves them… depending on how you look at it." He rocked on his heels.

"Why don't we all have a seat? I've ordered a fresh pot of tea as well as refreshments. I do believe we will be taking residence in the parlor for some time," Lady Southridge interjected.

As Neville and Beatrix took a seat, Curtis found his own and took a deep breath.

"Do share your news." Lord Neville leaned forward, resting his elbows on his knees.

"Miss Lamont, have you ever heard of a gentleman by the name of Sir Lambert Kirby?" he asked, studying her expression carefully.

"No," she answered.

"You?" Curtis turned to Neville.

"No, I'm afraid not. Who is he?" Neville clipped, his gaze darting to Beatrix and back.

"That's the rub. According to him and to certain documentation presented at his local magistrate then brought to London, he is your cousin, Miss Beatrix. The son of your father's brother and, that being said, claims he has documentation that would include him in your father's estate through marriage to one of the daughters of the late baron," Curtis finished quietly.

"Pardon?" Beatrix asked, her face a mask of confusion.

"The bastard says he has the right to marry you to attain your fortune," Lord Neville spoke through clenched teeth.

"Well, that is absurd," she murmured quietly, her shoulders rigid. "My father did not speak with his brother. They were estranged. He died without an heir before my mother and father. And he certainly did not make a marriage contract between this… gentleman and myself."

"Miss Lamont, while I have not seen the documentation, that such a claim has passed from the local magistrate clear to London leads to the assumption that there is some validity to his statement. However, you are correct on one point. The marriage stipulation is not for simply you, but *one* of the Lamont heirs."

Curtis waited for the weight of his words to settle. He swallowed, his gaze shooting to Neville and back to Beatrix as she began to speak. "But Bethanny is married, so that would leave myself and Berty, but she is far too young—"

"To be married immediately, yes…" He let the words linger.

He saw understanding dawn on her face. "They could force her into a contract with a stranger? She's only ten!"

"Indeed, but contracts can be drawn up at birth, Miss

Lamont. It is odd, not common anymore, and such a contract couldn't be forced, but there would certainly be pressure — unwanted and persistent. Based on what we know, Sir Kirby wouldn't hesitate to stalk you or your family."

"This is preposterous. And this is with the assumption that this, this Kirby gentleman is even valid in his assertion!" She stood and began pacing.

"Let us address a separate question for a moment. You said that there was no reason to continue her ruse because her whereabouts were already known. How did his happen? Especially when it took me quite a while to discover the truth myself," Lord Neville asked, his tone brusque and businesslike.

"It would seem that Sir Kirby has been scouring the countryside as well — rather, his men have been. It was only a matter of time, Neville. So while her whereabouts aren't known, they are certainly on a short timeline."

"Damn," he swore quietly.

"So, if I'm understanding this correctly, Sir Kirby is out scouring the countryside for me, thinking he has the correct documentation to prove that I'm destined to be his wife — archaic as it is — all so he can inherit my family's fortune. And if I refuse, then there's a chance that my little sister could be stalked with the same intention?" Beatrix paused in her pacing, her gaze darting between Neville and Curtis.

"That about sums it up. Yes." Curtis nodded once then stood. "But that doesn't mean that it is set in stone. He has no power to enforce anything at this point."

"Which works in our favor." Neville stood as well, a determined gleam in his eye, one that was both frightening and assuring all at once.

"Exactly."

"What if... what if we give him what he wants?" Neville paused, his gaze locking with Curtis, full of implication and meaning.

"You mean—"

"Yes."

"And then—"

"Quite possibly."

"We'll have to move quickly."

Neville snorted. "Is there another way?"

"Not that I can imagine. Is she up to it?" Curtis' gaze flicked to Beatrix then back to Neville in question.

"Yes," Neville answered decidedly.

"Am I up to what? For heaven's sake, gentlemen, will you please explain yourselves?" Beatrix's voice interrupted.

"I do think that there's no other option." Lady Southridge stood as well. Curtis had quite forgotten she was present, let alone imagined she had followed such an odd conversation.

"Am I the only one who has *not* gone mad?" Beatrix threw her hands down in a frustrated gesture.

"You, my dear, are going to London," Lady Southridge explained in a quiet tone, motherly even.

"Why?" It was a simple word, but Curtis could hear the confusion and pain laced within. For a moment, he thought of Maria. How would she feel in this situation?

How would he feel if he were in Neville's?

His blood boiled at the thought of some other man claiming what was his, and he wondered how Maria had responded to his letters. He had taken care not to write them in a similar fashion, but still, there was always a chance.

If she did suspect? How did she feel about it?

"Because you have a wedding to plan." Neville spoke darkly, pulling Curtis from his musings and back to the present.

"A wedding? You cannot mean for me to marry Sir Kirby—" Beatrix took a step forward, her face pinched with hurt.

"Bloody hell, you are! You're marrying me. I do believe I've explained that enough the past few days. You truly are difficult on my ego, Miss Lamont." A small smile tipped the corner of his mouth, and Curtis glanced away, not wanting to be part of what was surely a private exchange.

"I'm… confused."

"We're going to continue the ruse, only in a different manner…" Neville started.

"Oh heavens, no more *Bev!*" she all but cried.

"It wasn't that bad," Lady Southridge replied, her tone slightly offended.

Beatrix shot her a glare.

"No, no more *Bev.* You'll be Miss Lamont, but you're going to buy us some time with the ruse that you're open to the idea of marrying Sir Kirby," Curtis replied.

"No."

"Yes." Neville took a step toward her.

"No." She lifted her foot and brought it down with a hard thump.

"Did she just stomp?" Curtis asked, amused, but she paid him no mind. Her gaze was in a battle with that of Neville's.

"Yes. Because we need to solve this if you wish to ensure that you and your sister are completely free. This is the easiest and most viable solution. Curtis and I will address everything else, but we need time. Can you give us that, Beatrix?" Curtis glanced to Lady Southridge at the way Neville used Miss Lamont's Christian name so freely, but she didn't seem fazed.

Dear Lord, if that would have happened in London the world would have stopped spinning!

"Yes," Beatrix whispered.

Lord Neville closed his eyes and nodded once. "Thank you."

"There will be no shortage of sparks with you two, will there?" Curtis noted, uncomfortable with the exchange.

"You have no idea," Lady Southridge answered, her tone ironic.

"If you'll excuse me, gentlemen, I do believe I have to pack." Beatrix curtsied and turned to the door.

As she passed Lord Neville, he reached out and grasped her arm, pausing her exit. "We will get to the bottom of this, and you will *not* marry that man."

"See that your promise is not idle. Because my sister will not be forced into such an arrangement. If you truly are set on my hand, you have no other option."

Curtis raised his brows at such a brave remark, given so determinedly to one of London's most reclusive and powerful men. At once, he decided that she was indeed worthy of his friend. She would be no wallflower, no fainting miss.

Lady Southridge quietly excused herself as well, following Miss Lamont, and Curtis was thankful for the time to speak candidly with his friend and colleague. They had much to discuss. Much to plan. And time was of the essence.

And the sooner he got back to London, the better.

For more reasons than one.

# Chapter Eleven

IT WAS DECIDED that Lady Southridge and Miss Lamont would leave for London in a day's time, giving Curtis and Neville the opportunity to arrive there before them, taking care not to raise any suspicion. As the two made their way back to the city, they reviewed the plans they'd made the night before.

"If you only understood." Neville sighed heavily as he leaned against the velvet cushion of the richly appointed carriage.

Curtis considered Neville's words.

Rather, considered them again.

It would be hell. Utter and complete hell. To have Maria and know that there was a very real and possible threat… it was unthinkable.

"I cannot imagine," Curtis replied.

"Because you've been so close to marriage that a house party has enticed you to sacrifice your bachelor status on the altar of matrimony?" Neville replied with a cold tone, his eyes flashing open with bitterness.

"No, I cannot say I've had the pleasure of being so… enticed," Curtis lied. There was no reason to enlighten his friend, not when he had so much else to deal with.

Neville cocked his head, studying him. Damn it all, he knew.

"Liar." Neville narrowed his eyes. "I must say, the idea of you, a dedicated bachelor in every sense, entertaining the notion of—"

"You do realize that your possessive behavior earlier cannot be repeated once we leave this estate?" Curtis interrupted, trying to change the subject.

Neville opened his mouth then closed it, tilting his head before answering. "I'm mindful."

"You cannot even be seen with her." Curtis took it a step further. "It could jeopardize the entire operation."

"I'm bloody aware!" Neville all but shouted and, turning away, ran his fingers through his hair. "Hell… this is hell. Do we have anything on this Kirby bastard?"

"There's speculation, but—"

"Speculation doesn't produce results," Neville finished.

"Exactly."

"There's no other party that could have a motive to raise a threat against the Lamont sisters. Surely, he is behind—"

"That's the idea, the speculation, but without proof…" Curtis let the phrase linger.

"We could create a carriage accident." Neville spoke in a low threat.

"And undermine your integrity? My integrity? No. And you wouldn't even if you had the opportunity."

Neville snorted. "I'm just thankful we have some sort of plan." He pinched the bridge of his nose. Surely, the poor man was on the brink of madness.

"We have to work quickly to discredit Kirby's claim. You know that as soon as Beatrix is known to be in London, he'll be sniffing around her skirt. And with her directions to appear amicable to his suit…" Neville's tone grew dark.

"True, but women require wooing, do they not? He'll not expect her to agree to his suit immediately, especially with his claim still being validated before the regent."

"Heavens above, I hope so. Surely, that would buy us some time. Do you know if he is currently a man of means, or is his only claim to fortune that which belongs to the Lamonts?" Neville growled.

"From what I can understand from my sources, he is not a man of means, but neither is he destitute. I left Henry with the express instructions to follow him upon my departure. I sincerely hope that he has additional information upon our arrival to London."

"Henry? Do you think he's up to the task?" Neville asked, his tone dubious.

"Yes. The lad has proven himself quite capable in the past few months. I felt it was a wise choice."

"Lad? The boy's nearly eighteen." Neville shook his head. "When did that become so young to us? Are we truly that old?"

"I'm not certain about myself, but you, being of the ripe old age of thirty and one…"

"Bastard. You're only a year younger," Neville replied with no heat, simply an irritated grimace.

"My wager is when this whole nightmare is over, and you are indeed the victor of the fair maiden's hand…" Curtis waved his hand in a theatrical fashion. "…you two will create some sort of scene that will become the stuff of legends… some social faux pas that will forever shatter your reclusive lord status. I only hope I can have a front-row seat."

"That status served me well."

"Perhaps, but it's time for its end."

"I'm well aware."

"Then let us toast to the future and find our beds. Surely tomorrow will be upon us quickly, and we have much to do, old man."

"In truth, we do." Neville glanced outside at the passing countryside. "And let us pray our victory comes swiftly."

"To a happy and quick ending." Curtis nodded.

"To the end of Kirby's lies."

# Chapter Twelve

Time passed slowly as Maria fairly vibrated with both anxiety and expectation for the three days to pass. Finally, mercifully, they did, and she awoke with the delighted awareness that today she'd see Curtis. At first, as she came to realization of her admirer's identity, she didn't quite know how to feel and especially how to act. Did she tell him? Did she pretend she didn't realize? Did she simply go on as if the earth hadn't shifted? Yet today, today the very air was thick with expectancy, and even though she didn't quite know how she'd react, she was simply thrilled with the knowledge that she was wanted.

And possibly loved.

And she was quite taken with the gentleman doing the loving and wanting.

As her bare feet slid from her blankets and rested on the cold wooden floor, she bit her lip, trying to imagine all sorts of scenarios. Which was lovely. As odd as it sounded, it was quite fantastic to simply have someone to dream about, and have that someone have a face.

After ringing for Lottie, she smiled to herself as she selected her pale blue day dress and waited patiently as Lottie meticulously brushed her hair then began braiding, allowing gentle curls to frame her face. Her mind wandered as Lottie finished, and she had quite the scandalous thought! What if she kissed him? Her face heated at nearly the thought, but… it was an intriguing idea. How would he react? Would she dare be so bold?

Then she considered, what if she gave him a bit of his own medicine? How would he react if she were to pretend indifference to the admirer? Would he give himself away with a reaction?

"Miss, you're quite flushed. Are you well?" Lottie's voice interrupted her schemes.

Maria gently touched her throat and glanced down to her lap. "Of course. Just waking up still." She glanced up and gave Lottie a sleepy smile.

"Very well, miss. You're set. Is there anything else you'd be needing?" Lottie asked in her faint cockney accent.

"No. I'll be down shortly to break my fast with Mother."

"Oh, miss. Your mother already left this morning. She had an errand on Bond Street. Surely, she'll be back by tea time."

Maria shrugged slightly. "Very well. Thank you." And with a smile, she dismissed her maid and struggled to return to her daydreams, only to find that she couldn't quite focus. The thrilling anticipation was now growing into a bit of an anxiety. *Drat.*

She needed chocolate.

With a determined stride, she exited her room and strode down the hall, making her way to the dining room. She poured herself a steaming cup, the scent inviting and warm. Immediately, her nerves calmed as she selected several slices of buttered toast and took a seat. She dipped the toast in the hot chocolate and savored each bite.

"Miss?" Maxwell's voice drew her attention from her favorite breakfast.

She wiped her mouth with a linen napkin and turned. "Yes?"

"Mr. Sheppard is here. I've explained that you do not normally receive callers this early in the day—"

"But I'm sure he didn't listen, did he?" Maria arched a brow at Maxwell's irritated expression.

"No. No, I did not." Curtis strode into the breakfast room, patting Maxwell on the back once, earning a scathing glare from the butler.

Maria blinked, then a warm grin spread across her face and heated her entire body. She had always thought him devastatingly handsome, but now… now he was even more alluring and intimidating. She swallowed her sudden anxiety when his blue eyes crinkled as he grinned at her.

Dear Lord, how was she going to do this?

"I trust you've been well?" Curtis asked, taking a seat at the table and relaxing as if he hadn't a care — or secret — in the world.

Maria found her voice and sat as well. "Mostly." She gave a small hitch of her shoulders.

Maxwell shifted behind her chair, and the slight noise reminded her of his presence. She turned in her chair to face him. "Mr. Sheppard is a kind friend. There's not need to play guardian, Maxwell."

"Miss…" His tone was uneasy.

"The door is wide open, and we're sitting very properly apart at a breakfast table," Maria replied with some exasperation in her tone.

Maxwell narrowed his eyes as his gaze cut to Curtis then

back to Maria. "Very well, miss. I'll not be far." He glanced back to Curtis as he made the statement.

"Now, how was your trip out of London?" Maria asked, raising her cup of chocolate and hiding behind it slightly.

"Productive." He grinned. "I thought I was rather clever in getting that note to you."

"Shhh..." Heat flooded Maria's face. "Don't say that out loud!" she whispered harshly.

Curtis simply grinned, leaning closer. "I was very scandalous and wrote an unmarried lady a letter."

Maybe it was his grin.

Maybe it was the fact that he seemed so sure that he was still keeping his secret, but something gave Maria a wicked thought of her own.

"Well, unattached at the moment." She shrugged, taking a sip of her chocolate and setting it down.

"Ah, I assume you received more correspondence from Miss Lockett." His gaze took on a sharp glint, one that was slightly overconfident.

"Indeed. But not only that." Maria inclined forward, widening her eyes with just enough excitement to hopefully make it look real.

It worked, and Curtis leaned in as well, his gaze slightly guarded.

"I happened to meet Miss Lockett." She gave a wink and sat back, smiling broadly.

It was only a fraction of a moment, but Curtis' eyes widened before he recovered, a slightly forced grin on his face. "You *met* her?"

"Yes." Maria nodded. "She is quite... interesting. Fascinating really. I do believe that we are going to get along quite well." She let the words linger, their hidden meaning permeating the air.

"And, just where did you meet… *her?*" Curtis absently tugged on his cravat, his gaze sharp.

"Here."

"In the breakfast room?" His brow furrowed as his gaze darted about the room.

"No. I was receiving callers and well… she let herself be known." She gave a delicate flick of her wrist.

"She… let herself be known," he repeated.

"Yes. I expect I shall have an announcement soon." She gave him her brightest smile, watching as he visibly paled.

Yet she took pity on him when he had no response. Rather, he opened his mouth, seeming to speak, then closed it and glanced away.

"What? Are you not excited for me? Isn't this fantastic news?" she asked, tone bright.

"Yes." He blinked then collected himself. "Yes! Of course, I'll be the first to offer you congratulations on your happy event."

Maria rolled her eyes.

"I'm sincere!"

"But…" Maria toyed with her toast, taking a slow breath.

"But?" Curtis asked with expectation in his tone.

"…but… part of me… it feels attached to another." She gave him a hesitant glance. She was not quite sure where she was going with this… but she was slowly gathering ideas.

"Another, you say?" Curtis rested his elbows on the table and watched her with unabashed interest.

"Yes," Maria confessed.

"That's quite the quandary." Curtis nodded sagely.

"It is." She sighed. "But I don't think he could ever have feelings for me. If only…"

Curtis' gaze increased in its intensity. "If only…"

"You mustn't laugh," she warned, marveling at her own bravery.

But what was love if not brave?

And truly, that's what this could — would be. What, in many ways, it already was. Love. It had always been Curtis. She had just kept the secret from herself.

"I swear, I will not laugh." Curtis' brow furrowed.

"If only there was a way… to tell. To discern if this gentleman I'm attached to feels the same."

She stood from the table and started toward the hall. "Walk with me? I find I'm far too anxious to simply sit and do nothing." She gave him her most persuasive smile, hoping he'd follow. With any luck, he'd answer her question, mentioning a kiss. And if she were to be brave enough to attempt it, she wanted privacy.

Not the breakfast room where any servant could walk in at any moment.

This, her first kiss… she wanted all to herself. Sharing with no one, except Curtis.

Her heart hammered as he stood and proceeded to walk by her side. Once they were into the hall, she started to lead them toward the library. The servants cleaned it first, and so it would be vacant by this time of the morning. It wasn't perfectly private, but it was as secluded as she could get within her home, aside from her own chambers.

Curtis had remained oddly silent, and as she turned to glance at his face, he was watching her, his clear blue eyes studying her with a wary hope visible that left her breathless.

"There are many ways to discern a person's affection," he murmured intimately. His lips were captivating as they moved, drawing her attention.

She glanced away, pulling her wits about herself and gesturing to the library door. He nodded then followed her inside. The sound of the door clicking shut caused her to spin on her heel.

He slowly released the doorknob and walked toward her, his gaze intense and resolute, causing her heart to hammer as he slowed his stride and paused a breath away from her. The air was spicy with warmth that radiated from him as he glanced from her eyes to her lips and back.

"However, I do believe that the best way to discern…" He inched forward, trailing his nose along her jawline and exhaling cool air across her neck. "…is with a kiss."

His tone was so light she almost missed his words in the roaring noise of her beating heart.

"A kiss?" she breathed the words, closing her eyes and savoring the sensation of his hand slowly lacing with hers.

He nipped tenderly at the flesh along her jaw and slowly drew away. She could feel his heat recede, even though she hadn't opened her eyes yet. Then, just as she was about to open them, she felt the softest warmth against her lips. It was a hint of a touch, then he kissed her once more, this time lingering a moment longer before he slowly drew away. Maria willed her heart to slow its frantic beating, wanting to savor every moment, every touch.

She needed more.

And when he didn't kiss her again, she opened her eyes, meeting his slightly guarded gaze.

"Why did you stop?" she asked before she could consider her words.

A grin started in his eyes then spread to his face, his gaze darting to her mouth and back. But this time she met him halfway, pressing her lips to his, mimicking his movements.

She raised her hands and laced her fingers through his hair, marveling at his soft curls and tugging at them gently, wanting to feel more. Wanting to savor this brand new and thrilling sensation.

Curtis leaned into her, pulling her in tightly as he released her hand and wrapped his arms around her till even the air between them was gone. "Me. Dear Lord, say that the one you wanted was me." He broke from their kiss to plead for the answer then gently nipped at her lips.

"It was always you," Maria confessed, biting her lip as she waited for his reaction.

He slowly grinned, reaching around and trailing a finger down her nose and tracing her lips. "Truly?" he asked, his blue eyes marveling as they roamed her face.

"Possibly." She shrugged, her tone breathless even as she tried to flirt needlessly.

He claimed her lips quickly, silencing any other words she might have endeavored to say. Warm and inviting, his tongue tasted her lower lip, causing her to gasp in astonishment and pleasure.

"Dear Maria," he crooned against her lips before he took them captive once more.

Half of her waited expectantly for him to say something more, but it was as if he *showed*, rather than spoke the words. His kiss turned far more urgent, far more possessive as his lips left hers and trailed down her jaw to her neck as his hands caressed and mapped each curve within reach. Heart pounding, she lost all thought, save the deep and resounding thirst for more of his wicked attention.

But then he stopped.

As her eyes fluttered open, her brow furrowed with confusion, then horror. Had she done something wrong?

True, she was inexperienced but… what had caused him to so abruptly halt his passionate attentions? Was it her? A lifetime of insecurity crept up and washed over her like a rogue wave.

"Who… who was Miss Lockett?" His gaze narrowed slightly, as if confused by the emotions playing across her face.

"Oh…" Maria glanced to the side, a shy smile creeping in to place. "…that."

"Yes… *that.*" His brows drew together in a hint of suspicion.

"Well," she hedged, slowly meeting his gaze.

It took a moment, but she could verily see the way he started to connect everything in his expression before he narrowed his eyes even further and gave her the most shocked smile. "You minx," he spoke in a hushed tone, his smile shifting into more of a mischievous grin.

"Yes?" She blinked, feigning innocence.

"You knew," he spoke, his tone astonished, matching his expression.

"Knew… what… exactly?" She leaned forward and placed a soft kiss to his welcoming lips.

"How?" he asked, kissing her once more, lingering before withdrawing and cradling her face in his hands.

She shrugged slightly.

"Oh, no. I want to know where I slipped up." A tiny crease appeared in his brow as he frowned, thinking. "Was it the two letters I sent last?"

"No," she replied archly, a smile toying with her lips.

He twisted his lip slightly. "Was it the name? Lockett was my mother's maiden name, you know."

"Oh, I actually wasn't aware of that. Though, I probably

could have discovered that had I the inclination to research." She brazenly slid her arms up his chest slowly, watching as his expression of deep thought shifted to an expression of deep desire.

"You're trying to distract me." He grinned then leaned forward and playfully nipped at her neck, causing a gasp to escape her lips.

"Never." She spoke breathlessly.

He chuckled against her neck. "Did someone give me away?"

"No, your secret was safe with whomever you entrusted it," she answered sincerely.

"You're driving me bloody crazy," he murmured against her neck before leaning back and meeting her gaze once more. "How? I was so careful. Was it the day of the tulips? Was I too interested in them?"

Laughter bubbled out of her as she shook her head. "No, but it was that same day," she hinted.

"Perhaps you should work for the Crown. Good Lord. You're far more discerning than I ever expected." He chuckled. "What was it? I give up." He leaned in and kissed her softly then gasped. "The list." He slowly retreated and shook his head at her knowing smile.

"Finally," she answered with a giggle. "I had my suspicions, but it wasn't until I compared the last letter with the list that I could clearly see the—"

"Similarities of the writing," he finished.

"Similarities? They were identical." She reached up and cupped his face with her hand, the warmth of his skin melting through her glove.

"Damn and blast, I hadn't thought of that." He shook his head in wonder.

"Obviously," she retorted with a grin.

"Diabolical." He touched her nose with his finger, grinning.

"I prefer thoroughly observant." She hitched a shoulder. "But what of you? Why didn't you just…" She glanced away, insecurity flooding back like a late tide. "Why didn't you just tell me? Why go through such an elaborate ruse to pursue me?" She tilted her head, studying him.

"Ah, Maria." He took a deep breath and glanced to the door, then back to her. "It's a long story, one without a happy ending, I'm afraid." He led her to a sofa and sat beside her, never once letting go of her hand.

She nodded silently, waiting.

His story may not have had a happy ending, but she was bound and determined that their story… it would have the happiest of endings ever.

# Chapter Thirteen

Curtis tried to rally his thoughts, but like untamed horses, they tried to gallop into a hundred different directions. More than anything, he simply wanted to kiss Maria once more, picking up where they'd left off before he so quickly put the pieces together in his head.

She knew.

Bloody hell, how had she done that?

It was both terrifying and delightful to have the secret no longer a secret, but with one revelation came another.

And while he didn't think Maria would begrudge his fears because of his family history, he wasn't totally certain he would be easily forgiven for such extremes either.

So it was with great difficulty and Herculean self-control that he forced himself to only hold her hand, when he wanted to pull every inch of her so tightly against him that no even air separated them. As he glanced up to meet her gaze, he took a fortifying breath, forcing his body to retreat from its persisting demands.

"My parents created the most bloody and devastating civil war imaginable — without ever drawing a sword. I watched, from a young age, each of them systematically destroy the other. Betrayal is one thing, but when someone takes your most secret weakness and displays it for the world to see, and mocks you, one does not survive such humiliation. And when that humiliation isn't a one-time event…" Remembering, he relived the memories of his parents' conniving and how they would use him as bait, a casualty of their war. "It wasn't enough that my father had destroyed my mother's reputation in revenge of her betrayal. No. That was simply the first battle in a series of scrimmages that never actually ended. Every word, every move, every thought was careful and tactical, meant to slowly destroy the other." Curtis paused, watching as her wide and innocent eyes blinked in shock and what looked like pain.

"I can't even imagine," she replied, glancing down to their entwined fingers, squeezing his tenderly. "If they hated each other so much, why not simply divorce? True, neither would survive the effect on their social status, but if they had already been so reckless in that area…" She let the question linger.

"Because that is where it gets twisted, my love." He shook his head, his body heavy with the memories. "Because if they were free, then they could go their separate ways. No more need for war. They wanted the war, Maria. They hated each other so completely that they wanted to stay in the marriage, so that they could have free access to destroying the other." He spoke the words slowly.

"Dear God," she breathed. She lifted a dainty hand and covered her mouth in horror.

"And that is why I, until now, have never pursued a woman toward marriage. And why…" He shifted slightly so that was facing her completely. "…I went through such a roundabout means to try and pursue you, though I must admit that I didn't get as far with it as I was intending, you being such a prolific detective," he added with a smile, though his body remained tight with tension.

"I see. Curtis... I cannot even imagine." She glanced down to the floor. "I don't understand how a person could hate someone so completely."

"It's rather odd, but it didn't happen overnight. You see, they weren't a love match, but my parents did become friends. I never witnessed this, but in order for me to be present, then some sort of, at least, tolerance for each other had to exist. Cook told me all this when I was old enough to ask questions... and understand answers. But you see, one thing, one betrayal — even small — led to a sort of eye-for-an-eye mentality. Rather than move on, they gouged out a punishment on the other. And rather than admitting to a fault when they did do something wrong, they justified their actions, condemning the other one. So, slowly it grew. Starting small till it became their entire universe. It imploded one night when my father found my mother sitting in his office. When she didn't respond to his request for her to leave, he looked closer, noticing she wasn't moving. She had drunk the entire contents of his brandy cabinet — his prized vintage — and never woke up. He didn't attend her funeral, but spent every moment completely intoxicated. It wasn't more than a week later that he fell over dead."

"I see." Maria took a hesitant breath.

What he wouldn't give to know her thoughts! Her gaze met his, glanced away in thought, then met his once more, this time her green depths resolute.

"You do?"

"Indeed," she murmured. Maria reached up and tenderly caressed his jaw. Had she any idea how her touch affected him? It was akin to lightning on a dark night, illuminating his world to the extreme and jolting his body awake in ways he didn't know were possible.

Bloody hell, if this was what a touch did to him, he almost shuddered in desire at the thought of her doing more… touching.

His body hardened painfully at the mere thought.

Yet he forced his attention back into line as she spoke.

"You're quite brave, you know."

Her words surprised him. Shocked him, actually. Brave? Well, he supposed he was brave. After all, he did work for the Crown. But in this particular aspect of life? Love? He felt nothing but a coward, especially considering how he went about pursuing her.

"Bravery has many forms," he hedged, not wanting to admit his utter and complete lack.

"No." She shook her head slightly.

The movement sent a soft breeze of floral scent that electrified his senses.

"You endured a horrific and deplorable childhood. Few men, if any, would ever consider the idea of love… yet here you are." She slowly slid her hand down his jawline, caressing his neck then resting on his shoulder before placing her gloved hand at his heart. "Risking everything… for me." She blinked, her eyes glassy with emotion.

Dear Lord, was she crying? Helplessness flooded him as he tried to think of a way to comfort her.

"It's the most beautiful and romantic gesture, and I don't feel worthy of such a risk… but know this." She leaned forward and pressed the softest of kisses to his waiting lips, driving him mad with the intense desire to savor her delightful flavor far more deeply than she intended. She sighed across his lips. "Your heart is safe with me."

It was such a simple phrase. Easily spoken, flippantly if wished, yet the gravity of her words and the depth of meaning behind them overwhelmed him, set him free.

"Maria…" He murmured her name, his lips capturing hers in a gentle kiss of wonder. "…I swear on my own life that your heart is safe with me as well — should you ever bless me with the honor of capturing it." He added the last part in a bit of a rush, realizing that he hadn't actually made anything official.

And that was something that needed to be remedied immediately.

"Is your father home?" he asked between kisses, plans formulating in his mind.

"If not, he will be soon."

Curtis could taste her smile as she pressed into the kiss.

He pulled away briefly. "I have something…" He kissed her again deeply, searchingly. "…something to ask him… quite important, you see." He pressed into her once more, rejoicing as she willingly reclined onto the sofa, her soft frame welcoming him.

"Oh? And what would that be?" She twined her fingers through his hair, rendering him speechless, thoughtless, as he plundered her mouth, primal need threatening to overtake him.

Her body sang for him; he could hear it in the way her hips arched into his frame… the way her arms held him tightly… in the erratic breathing and beating of her heart…

A part of his mind registered footsteps; another part observed the door creak open, but both of them noticed the loud gasp that followed. Unapologetically, he slowly rose from his deliciously reclined position and held out a hand for Maria to do the same, a deep blush erupting across her beautiful face.

"I — I…"

Lady Moray's stutters pulled him from his drunken passion, and an unapologetic grin spread across his face. "I expect that Lord Moray is home?"

Lady Moray's expression sharpened immediately. "Yes."

"Brilliant. I do believe I have a very important matter to discuss. I'm sure it won't be long." He turned to offer a secretive smile at Maria, who was still suffering from embarrassed silence, though he did notice a mischievous gleam in her eye as she watched him.

"Perhaps you both would wait for me? I'm sure your daughter… the-soon-to-be Mrs. Sheppard… has much to discuss with her mother." At Lady Moray's gasp, he took the moment of their distraction to stand and bow. He needed to leave before they had a chance to notice his aroused state, so he quickly passed through the door and into the hall, Lady Moray's voice floating after him.

"His office is that way," she offered in a bewildered tone.

He slowly strode in the direction of Lord Moray's study, focusing on cold lakes and anything else that would alleviate his current state. He wanted every wit about him when he sealed his future, his future with Maria.

With a grin, he knocked on the door, eager for his destiny.

# Chapter Fourteen

MARIA BIT HER lip as she waited for the carriage to arrive at the Lyledell house. It was only a few days ago that Curtis had declared himself and scandalously imposed himself as a soon-to-be son-in-law. Her mother quickly forgave their... indiscretion, as soon as the proper arrangements had been made, and she hadn't stopped planning the wedding since. Of course, that the *banns* hadn't been read was a small detail, the only force strong enough to rein her mother in from shouting it to the world.

With a smug grin, Lady Moray met Maria's gaze from across the carriage. "I knew it," she said for the thousandth time.

And truthfully, Maria had to give her that concession. She had suspected Curtis' intentions far before she had, odd that.

As the carriage stopped in front of the grand staircase, Maria was immediately swept up into the vibrant Society that was London's *le bon ton*. Curtis was attentive as always, his secret grins a constant delight as he would always scandalously touch her hip or caress her hand when he thought no one was watching. Or perhaps he simply didn't give a whit. How she loved him!

"Care to dance? I have it on good authority that the next song will be a waltz." He grinned dangerously, and her insides burned with a smoldering heat.

"Of course." And sure enough, as the music began, it was, indeed, a waltz.

"Have I told you how utterly delicious you look tonight?" Curtis spoke seductively as he pulled her in far too close.

"Once or twice. At least this time, you'll notice what color of dress I'm wearing," she spoke archly.

"I always noticed," he replied sharply, though his eyes danced. "I merely forced myself to not look too closely. A man has only so much willpower. I had to ignore you if I was to keep my sanity at all." He smiled, all traces of his parents' legacy erased from his expression.

"You did not ignore me." Maria rolled her eyes slightly at his overreaction.

"Ha! That's where you're wrong. I did, and it was very difficult to not notice how your waist is the perfect shape for my hand…" He squeezed his hand slightly, emphasizing his point. "Or the way your height is perfect for stealing a kiss…" He leaned forward as if about to attempt to do so in the middle of the ballroom.

Maria leaned back, narrowing her eyes. She didn't want to cause that much of a scandal. When they were married, that would be different. Married. In time, she would be Mrs. Curtis Sheppard. A mere sir, he wasn't titled, but never had it mattered to her. Anyway, she would much rather marry for love.

And she was certainly getting her preference!

"Afraid?" he asked, pulling her thoughts back to the present.

"Of?"

"Me?" he replied darkly.

"No more than usual." She bit her lip and glanced away, noticing for the first time a dark-haired beauty who looked vaguely familiar.

Curtis must have followed her gaze. "That is Miss Beatrix Lamont." He answered her unasked question.

"The Duke of Clairmont's ward?" she asked, immediately recognizing the familial resemblance with Beatrix's sister, the more well-known Bethanny — though now she was Countess Graham. "Has she had a come out yet?"

"No."

"Who is the man she's with?" Maria immediately felt a chill at the way the man paid his partner no attention yet held her dangerously close. It was odd.

"Sir Kirby. The one I mentioned," he replied with slight insinuation.

"Ah. That would be why I don't recognize them."

The waltz ended, and Curtis excused himself, his gaze focusing on something far away. Maria recognized the expression; it was his "*I notice something only a spy would see*" expression. She would have disregarded it, except her curiosity was piqued, so she navigated the ballroom in order to keep her eye on the lovely Miss Beatrix Lamont and the disturbing Sir Kirby.

Just when she was about to walk away, she noticed a tightening of Sir Kirby's hand on Miss Lamont's wrist, sending warning bells in her head. She took a hesitant step forward, not sure of what she would actually do to help, when a large footman barreled into Sir Kirby, knocking him to the floor and spilling lemonade all over his evening kit. The footman had effectively divided Miss Lamont from her unkind suitor, and she stood with her mouth covered with a dainty hand as she watched the scene unfold. Sir Kirby uttered a few harsh words and threats before storming off, and then the oddest flicker of recognition stretched across Miss Lamont's face, briefly appearing then gone, so that Maria almost missed it. She focused her attention to Sir Kirby's retreating back, and once he left the hall, she turned to look for Miss Lamont, but did not find her — nor the clumsy footman.

"Ready, love?" Curtis whispered in her ear, startling her.

"I think… Miss Lamont…" Maria frowned, turning to Curtis and then glancing back to where Miss Lamont was.

"She's in good hands… the best of hands, apart from mine, that is."

Understanding dawned, but rather than say the word, she simply nodded. Neville. A grin spread wide across her face. Curtis had shared enough of the story for her to put the pieces together, at least some.

"I suspect you'll be leaving early?" she asked with an arch to her brow.

"You know me well."

"Be safe," Maria spoke tenderly, feeling somewhat afraid.

"Always. After all, I have quite a busy future," Curtis replied, his gaze warm.

"Busy, horrifically and beautifully busy, and if so you so much as shorten that future by one day I swear I'll—"

He pressed finger to her mouth. "You have nothing to fear, love." He slowly removed the finger from her lips and pressed it to his own, then disappeared into the crowd.

Taking a deep breath, Maria willed for the party to end so that she might find her bed, find sleep, then find that the morning brought news of Curtis.

# Chapter Fifteen

"I don't know how we missed this," Curtis remarked with frustrated interest.

"To be honest, I wouldn't have thought of it if Beatrix — Miss Lamont — hadn't pointed me in that direction." Neville shook his head thoughtfully.

"For him to be after the duke? This entire time? It confounds me!" Curtis set aside the condemning parchment that was the key to the whole sordid mystery of Sir Kirby.

"But we have to act quickly, to strike while the iron is hot. He will not suspect that we have discovered his true identity… or intentions." Neville paced about the room, his heavy boots echoing softly against the wooden floor of his study.

"Indeed, but—" Curtis blew out a heavy sigh. "—I can hardly fathom it."

"I do believe that was the whole intention," Neville replied while shrugging into his great coat.

"One must admit that it is quite diabolical… brilliant, even." Curtis carefully tucked the document into a leather folder, pondering the twist the case had taken.

"I'm not one to offer up compliments to criminals."

Neville turned to face Curtis, his impatience evident in the clipped tone he used.

"Right." Curtis cleared his throat, slightly humbled but far too anxious to see the confrontation through to the end, to feel anything more.

"If you're quite finished complimenting the blackguard, shall we be away?" Neville gestured to the door with an unnecessary flourish of his hand.

Curtis simply shot him a dark look as he passed. "We'll take my curricle. It's still waiting outside from my arrival."

Once aboard the conveyance, Curtis snapped the leather straps, and the matched grays jumped at his command, pulling them out from Mayfair District and toward the residence of Sir Kirby. The London air was thick with the scent of impending rain.

"Of course it's going to downpour. We're in a curricle," Neville grumbled as he studied the heavy gray clouds.

"It will not," Curtis clipped, but his gaze darted upward.

Bloody London weather! They passed through the streets of Mayfair and into a lower, yet still respectable, social strata of the city. Curtis felt the swell of determination, of impending victory that normally surged through his veins at the end of a case. It was glorious, but it was… slightly incomplete. Because in the past, if something went wrong, he would perish doing something he loved, fighting for justice. And while noble, it was different now. Because of Maria. A twinge of fear tickled his mind, shocking him. He didn't want anything to go wrong… and it likely wouldn't, yet still. It was enough to make him pause.

"Thank the good Lord for Henry's directions. Look! There!" Neville gestured to a hired hack who had just pulled up before the entrance to Sir Kirby's lodgings.

Pulling the grays to the side, Curtis watched as two men exited the conveyance and approached the door. Both men were well-dressed and carried leather folders, much like the one Curtis clung to. "Barristers?" he asked.

"It would appear so. If that is the case, then fortune is on our side, my friend." Neville gave him a victorious smirk.

"Indeed." Curtis glanced behind them then pulled the grays back onto the road. He paused them before Sir Kirby's door.

After exiting the curricle, Neville bounded up the stairs, Curtis at his heels. After sharing a glance, Neville placed a solid knock on the large black door.

"Yes?" A young butler answered the door, his expression faltering as he took in the two men before him.

"We are here to have an audience with Sir Kirby. We have information that concerns his current state of affairs." Curtis was careful to keep a neutral and professional tone.

Indecision flickered across the butler's expression. "If you'll give me but a moment, my lords."

When the door closed, Neville spoke lowly, "Surely Kirby isn't as deep in the pocket as he'd like people to imagine if he cannot hire a proper butler. Surely, the man has little-to-no experience with the position."

"Indeed, he didn't even request our cards," Curtis murmured back.

"Which is to our benefit."

"Exactly."

The door opened, revealing the butler once more. "Sir Kirby is currently not available, but he bids you leave your card—"

"It would be in your employer's best interest if he were to—" Curtis started.

"Bloody hell with it all." Neville shoved the butler aside and strode down the dimly lit hall.

*Well, so much for neutrality!*

"Gentlemen! I must insist! You cannot simply—"

Curtis spun and gave a solid right hook to the butler's face, sending him sprawling to the floor, unconscious. His hand ached, but nothing overly terrible. Kicking the door completely shut, he dragged the butler's legs out of the way and turned to Neville.

"I don't know if that was necessary, but I do approve of the methodology." Neville nodded once.

A moment later, they paused before a closed door that muffled the voices within.

"Your case should be reviewed within the next week, sir—"

"That's too long! I don't have time for this!" Sir Kirby's voice rose.

"These things take time, sir. You must understand," another man spoke.

"So you've said! Far too many times for me to count!"

"This is a legal matter. Legal matters tend to require much patience as a thorough investigation must take place for something of this nature to even be considered altered in any way."

"I've given you every piece of documentation. It should be obvious to any fool who even glances at the evidence!"

"Have you heard enough?" Neville asked Curtis lowly.

"Indeed. Those gentlemen are the barristers conducting the case," Curtis answered.

In the silence, they heard the men speak once more. "We'll take our leave now and will check with you in a few days' time."

Quickly, Neville opened the door and strode in. Curtis followed close behind, glorifying in the horrified shock of Sir Kirby's face as he glanced from his unexpected visitors and then back to his legal counsel.

"Who the hell do you think you are?" Kirby stood, his face red with rage.

"That is a brilliant question," Curtis replied, a dry sarcasm lacing his tone.

"If that will be all, we will take our leave—" The two barristers stood, their expressions worried.

"No, I believe you'll wish to stay for this… introduction."

"Russell!" Kirby called, glancing behind the men.

"Your… capable butler is going to be nursing quite the headache in a few hours," Curtis replied with a calm tone, arching a brow daringly.

Neville circled the room, sizing up his opponent. "Do you know who I am?" Neville asked.

"No. And if I don't know you, then you must be nothing more than a common criminal," Kirby spat, glancing to the door as if evaluating his escape.

"That was unnecessary," Curtis replied, pretending offense.

*Oh, this is going to be good.*

"I know you!" One of the barristers took a step toward Curtis and Neville. "I never forget a face. And you — you're the one that solved that Prother case! I was on the floor when it was discussed. Neville, isn't it?" The man snapped his fingers, recognition lighting his expression.

"Ah, Prother… yes," Neville answered, his gaze faltering slightly. There were some things that a person would never leave in the past. And Curtis felt a sharp pang of empathy for his friend.

Kirby shot a mutinous glance at the barrister. "What has that to do with me?"

"Ironically, the similarities are substantial… but unrelated," Curtis interjected.

"Kirby… now that you know who I am… shall I tell others who *you* are?"

"They all know who I am!" Kirby shouted, but it was clear that his confidence was faltering.

"Now… I'm not quite so certain of that," Curtis replied.

"Nor am I… especially after I discovered a very telling secret." Neville strode right up to Kirby, who stood shaking, his hands in fists at his side, eyes narrowed.

Leaning in, Neville whispered, "I've never been good at keeping these types of secrets."

It was like a well-rehearsed act at Drury Lane. And Curtis watched with rapt attention, waiting for the fatal blow.

"You have no proof." Kirby attempted to call his bluff.

"Ha!" Curtis' outburst interrupted the stare down between Neville and Kirby.

"I don't understand," the older barrister spoke.

Perhaps it was time to end the cat-and-mouse game.

"May I?" Curtis asked, waiting for affirmation from his friend. At Neville's nod, he withdrew the document from his leather case.

"I have in my possession a verified copy of St. George's marriage registry from the year 1808, if you wish to authenticate." He went around to the barristers and displayed the document. "It states here that Sir Richard Kirby was, on the day of April 3, 1808, married to a woman by the name of Marianne Lamont Greene."

The air was suffocating. Curtis glanced to Kirby, watching as his color nearly drained. "And I have on the next page a document stating that Sir Kirby's wife met her end six months later."

"That proves nothing!" Kirby shouted.

"I'm failing to see the connection," the younger barrister questioned, his tone confused.

"We failed to see it at first as well," Neville answered, pacing before Kirby slowly, methodically. Each step was like the incessant dripping of water, agitating, threatening to drive one mad. It was bloody brilliant, as far as Curtis was concerned.

"It was never about the Lamont's fortune, was it?" Neville asked.

Kirby remained silent.

"It was about revenge," Neville spoke darkly. "A man with nothing to lose—"

"And everything to gain," Curtis finished, arching a brow, taking a menacing step toward his foe.

"You can't prove that," Kirby threatened.

"So you think… but I don't have to. I simply have to say one name… to one person." Neville spoke smoothly, his tone dangerously chilling.

"He wouldn't even remember her name," Kirby spat.

"But you remember his."

Kirby hissed.

"Tell me, did she threaten to leave you the week after you were married, or did she wait a whole month?" Curtis asked condescendingly, the swell of victory filling him as he watched Kirby's reaction, how he took the bait. "A week? Perhaps he couldn't—"

"Silence!" Kirby shouted, his chest heaving, his body tense.

"Ah, I think we struck a nerve." Curtis spoke triumphantly.

"Do you think she even told him she was married? I'd have to say no… because she was already planning on leaving you."

"She loved me. It was he! He poisoned her mind against me! She — she—"

"She wanted out. Away from you." Neville spoke the words with a deathly calm.

"He didn't even remember her! Didn't even attend her funeral when she died carrying his child!" Kirby yelled and swiftly threw over a table. "He'll burn in hell for what he did to me — to her!" The crystal glass of brandy that had been sitting on the table flew toward the hearth and shattered against the stone, spraying the brandy into the flames, causing them to burst forth with a bright and hungry explosion of fire.

"And since you, a mere sir, cannot think to compete with a duke… you sought the more patient route. His wards," Neville completed.

"And with your dead wife's middle name Lamont… you were able to easily falsify what was necessary to avoid question."

"Knowing that, even if it never happened, if you never got to his wards, eventually he'd have to face you."

"And then you'd have your final revenge."

"Did you really think you'd get away with murdering a duke?" Neville asked softly, but loud enough for the other barristers to hear, judging by their abrupt gasps.

"He would have known what it's like to suffer. His wife would have known *my* bloody pain," Kirby swore, his tone both angry and broken.

"Which is why you went to his residence every day at four o'clock in the afternoon."

"The very time your wife died," Curtis added.

"He never even knew she was increasing." Kirby spoke with venom.

"That's because she wasn't," Neville replied swiftly, pounding another nail in Kirby's proverbial coffin.

"If you had read the report, she died of an opiate overdose, no evidence of her… increasing."

"She lied to you," Curtis finished.

"No, she… she—"

"Lied," Neville finished.

"Liar falls for liar. Romantic, is it not?" Curtis studied his nails and brushed an imaginary speck of lint from his jacket, hoping that the more unaffected he appeared, the more it would drive Kirby into hot fury, causing additional slips.

Kirby's silence reigned in the room, acting as both his confession and his own awakening.

"In light of this new information…" The older barrister stood and cleared his throat. "…I do believe I need to summon a constable." He glanced to Neville then Curtis, and with their nod, he left.

"She loved me…" Kirby's tone was broken.

"No, but I do believe that you loved her," Neville allowed.

Curtis cut him a sympathetic glance. Never had he seen Neville show any empathy for a criminal.

"They'll hang me for sure," Kirby replied, his gaze frantically searching the room.

"You'll not escape." Curtis took a menacing step forward.

Kirby lunged for the door, but Neville knocked him to the floor with an upper cut to the jaw. Kirby stilled, unconscious.

Curtis nodded his approval. "Impressive."

"I cannot tell you how long I've wished to do that."

Neville stood and straightened his coat. "You," he called to the remaining barrister who stared at Kirby's body with wide-eyed shock, "find me something to tie him up."

"Y-yes, my lord."

Shortly after they tied Kirby's hands with some rope found in his desk, several constables arrived. Curtis quickly disclosed the proof and confession, with the barristers confirming every detail.

As Kirby's unconscious body was carried out the door, Curtis noticed that Neville was oddly still, his expression clouded, no doubt reliving his own past… painfully similar to what had just taken place. Thank the good Lord for Miss Beatrix Lamont. Neville deserved a love match. He placed his hand on his friend's shoulder. "Are you with us, old man?"

He blinked then turned as two constables approached.

"Pardon?"

"Is there anything you wish to add to Mr. Sheppard's statement?" one with a neatly trimmed mustache asked.

"No, no." Neville shook his head.

"Then I believe that's all we need. Er, what about the fellow in the front who's knocked out?"

"He's the butler. I'm not sure what role he played."

"We'll take him in as well then, just to gather his statement."

The officers left, and Curtis rubbed his hands together. "Our work here is done." He smiled.

# Chapter Sixteen

IT MIGHT HAVE been only a day, but it felt as if an eternity had ticked by in the process. Maria continued to wait for word on Curtis, but none was forthcoming. Her mother chalked her restlessness up to wedding anxiety, and Maria allowed her to believe it. Better that than worry that her soon–to-be son-in-law was pursuing a criminal.

*Dear Lord, is it always going to be like this?* Waiting, wondering… hoping. It wasn't that she didn't trust Curtis' skills, it was that, well, she didn't trust the criminal's desperation. It was a something to consider, something converse about later.

When he was back.

Safe.

"Maria, dear," her mother called from the other room, her voice jarring Maria's already-taut nerves.

"Yes?" Maria replied as kindly as possible — as possible through clenched teeth.

"I've spoken with your father and we've come to the conclusion that eight weeks' time would be an excellent date for the wedding. We'll have it at St. George's of course, as long as there is room on their docket. I'm sure your father can provide some… *incentive* if necessary to procure a date."

Her mother breezed into the library, her voice preceding her, giving Maria the chance to school her features. *Eight weeks? Two whole months?* True, it wasn't horrifically long as far as engagements were concerned. It was actually blessedly quick, but… well, looking forward through those fifty-six days seemed like an eternity.

Odd. Because she could easily remember fifty, even sixty days ago. And while it felt like a lifetime — seeing as she hadn't been aware of Curtis' intentions — it also seemed rather like a blink, paradoxically. Surely, that meant that time could, indeed, move quickly? Or was it simply vain hope.

She rather thought it was vain hope.

"Maria?" Her mother's tone caused her thoughts to snap back to attention.

"Yes?"

"Well?" Her mother blinked, her expression a cross between amusement and impatience.

She wanted to shout *no*, but in truth, what choice did she have but to agree? "Yes. That will be suitable." It wasn't glowing enthusiasm — and judging by the way her mother's mouth pinched, that what was she was looking for — but it was all Maria could muster.

"I'm assuming you'd rather be married much more expediently?" her mother asked, her gaze narrowing.

"Well, of course, but I understand—"

"Maria. Is there something that we need to know?" Lady Moray took a cautious pace toward her.

"Pardon?" Maria took a step back, slightly alarmed by her mother's sharp gaze.

"Is there a *reason* for the wedding to be sooner?" Her

mother glanced from Maria's face, to her belly, then back.

Then it clicked. "What? Heaven's no!" Maria felt her face blush crimson. Dear Lord, did the woman think that Curtis had compromised her?

Her mother nodded once, as if her daughter's deep blush was proof of her innocence. "Well, it's just that..."

Maria felt a thick dread wind about her consciousness. "Just that *what*, Mother?" she asked, even though she knew instinctively that she'd dislike the answer.

Lady Moray glanced away, smoothing an imaginary crease on a nearby brocaded chair. "It would simply explain why he was so quick to offer for your hand... seemingly out of the blue." She delicately shrugged, meeting her daughter's gaze unapologetically.

"What?" Maria gasped. Was this what her mother thought of her worthiness? That Mr. Sheppard would only offer for her if he *had* to?

"Don't be offended. It truly does make sense. Your father and I had wondered—"

"Even Father thought so?" Maria felt anger swell within her at the thought of her parents' opinion of her ability to make a match without resorting to loose morals.

Dear Lord.

"Calm yourself, Maria." Her mother gave an impatient sigh, as if chastising a toddler.

It was like a mirror flipped, showing the exact scene but from a reverse perspective. How often had Curtis mentioned that he didn't appreciate the way her mother treated her? She hadn't given it much thought, but to suddenly see everything from his perspective...

And to realize just how little hope they had for her to make a match on her own merit...

It was devastating.

It was freeing.

It was the bloody last straw.

"Mother," Maria began, straightening her shoulders and taking a few deliberate steps toward her, "never again will I tolerate you speaking to me in such a way. If my soon–to-be husband had heard even a fraction of this conversation…" She paused. "Tearing someone down doesn't mean you're fixing them. It simply means that you're an unkind and petty person."

Maria watched as Lady Moray's eyes widened. She wanted to believe that her mother had her best interests at heart, but there was doubt.

"And I'd appreciate it if you'd consider your words with more care, because while I don't want to think the worst of you, you are not assisting me in proving that correct."

At her mother's soft gasp, Maria quit the library and took the stairs quickly, heading straight for her room.

Eight weeks.

She'd just have to make it through one day at a time.

And it was with that thought that she picked up one of her favorite books and proceeded to read, willing the time to pass quickly.

And thankfully, it did. Less than an hour later, there was a knock on the door.

Her heart jumped with anxiety. Was it her mother? She feared the cutting reply her mother may have in response to her earlier show of backbone, yet she resolved to not give ground.

But it wasn't her mother.

It was Maxwell.

"Miss? Mr. Sheppard is here to see you."

Excitement flooded her limbs as she grinned and rushed out the door, not caring that it was anything but ladylike to take the stairs at such a pace, but the expression of delight on Curtis' face made her forget all else.

"Good day." He grinned broadly as she took the last step.

How she wanted to fling herself into his arms, but with difficult restraint, she held back and settled for extending her hand. Warm blue eyes met hers as he kissed her gloved hand, sending shivers of delight across her flesh, reminding her of the sensation of those lips on hers.

"How about a walk?" Maria asked abruptly, hearing her mother's entrance.

Curtis' brow furrowed for only a moment before readily accepting her invitation. Maria avoided eye contact with her mother, rather asked Maxwell to fetch Lottie to assist as chaperone. And in a few short minutes, they were taking slow steps toward Hyde Park, the maid in tow.

"Want to tell me what that was all about?" Curtis asked, lacing her arm around his own tightly, all but snuggling her into the lee of his body as they walked.

The heat that seeped off him was luxurious, along with the spicy, citrusy scent that permeated the air around him.

"I'm in a bit of a… battle of the wills with my mother."

"Oh." Curtis nodded once. "It's about time." He gave her a quick smile of approval.

"I was quite abrupt," Maria confessed.

"I'm sure you only spoke the truth."

"Yes. But well, the truth can hurt." She shrugged.

Curtis turned her toward him. "Only to those who aren't willing to hear it."

She bit her lip, debating. "She… she thought that the reason you offered for me was because…" Maria couldn't bring herself to say it. She should have just left well enough alone!

Even though she turned away slightly, she could still see his careful study of her person from the corner of her eye.

"I offered because…" He trailed off, and she glanced up to meet his gaze. His expression went from curious to furious in a moment. "No, she didn't think that I offered out of necessity, did she?" His expression already gave away that he expected the affirmative answer.

"Well, yes," Maria admitted.

"Bloody hell— Er… pardon my language." He shook his head, abruptly changing their direction, heading back to her residence.

"No!" Maria planted her feet, halting their progress. "Please. I already set it straight, but I cannot. Please. I don't want to relive that humiliation again." She spoke quietly, looking down and studying the cobbled path.

At Curtis' deep sigh she glanced up, watching as indecision flickered across his gaze. "Not now. I won't do anything about it… now. That is all I can promise." He took another deep breath, as if trying to calm himself.

"Thank you," said Maria, heartfelt.

He took her arm once more, snug against him, and turned toward the park.

"Tell me about your adventure." Curiosity thickened her tone.

Curtis grinned wryly, no doubt recognizing her attempt at changing the topic of conversation. "I'm pleased to say that there is no longer any threat to the duke or his wards — any of them!"

"Splendid! That is indeed fantastic news! Was it easier than you expected?" She watched, fascinated, as his expressions were animated and excited.

"In some ways. I had to punch a butler," he replied with a dry grin.

"Pardon?" She paused mid-step, blinking up at him.

"A butler. He was in my way." Curtis shrugged, as if getting into fisticuffs with the help was an everyday occurrence. "He was most unhelpful," he added, studying her with obvious amusement.

"Apparently. Remind me to always be quite helpful to you," Maria replied cheekily, still trying to wrap her mind around an altercation with a butler.

"It went smoothly after that. Providence was truly on our side with even the caliber of witnesses. Barristers." He shook his head as if still amazed by their good fortune.

"My," Maria answered. "Well, I'm very pleased that you are back safe and sound." She gave a quick smile and then glanced to the path before them, the south gate of Hyde Park growing closer with each step.

"Maria." Curtis spoke her name quietly, giving her pause.

She turned and watched as he opened his mouth, then clamped it shut, taking a determined step toward the gate.

Finally, he continued. "Let us find a place to sit a while. Isn't the weather lovely?"

Narrowing her eyes, she followed his lead toward an unoccupied bench not far through the gate, and at his behest, she sat beside him, keeping a respectable distance as Lottie watched from several paces away.

"What are you thinking about?" Maria asked, scrutinizing his face carefully.

"It was rather odd today." He took a deep breath and twined her fingers through his. He caressed her fingers playfully. "I found that while I relished the excitement of the chase, I didn't appreciate the danger it involved. Normally, the danger doesn't even give me pause, but today, it did." He met her gaze, his blue eyes deeply searching hers.

"I had my own hesitations today." Maria glanced away, taking a deep breath before turning back to him. "I did not like not knowing whether you were well or in danger. It was rather difficult."

"I see." Curtis nodded. "We need to have a conversation about my profession."

Maria glanced away, not entirely comfortable yet touched that he'd even consider her feelings. What gentleman of the *ton* would even ponder such a thing? Women with opinions were frowned upon. Or so her mother had mentioned — several times.

He reached up and tenderly grasped her chin in his hand, guiding her face back to his as he spoke. "You can be honest with me, Maria. Please understand. I value your honesty above almost all things."

The sincerity in his gaze was impossible to deny, and coupled with the knowledge of what had destroyed his parents, how could she be anything but utterly transparent in her thoughts? "I'm a war between the elation I feel at knowing you are doing something you love and the worry I feel pondering if you'll returned injured, or worse."

"I understand." He slowly released her chin. "I find I'm much more reluctant to take such risks as well. I propose a compromise." He caressed her hand once more, sending shivers of delight up her arm and spreading throughout her body like butterfly wings.

"What do you propose?"

He twisted his lips playfully. "That I only take the cases that you and I have agreed upon. Please understand I'll only be able to give minor details, but it will be enough that you can understand the risk. Is that acceptable?"

Maria considered his words, mulling over them. "Agreed. I find that is entirely acceptable." She responded to his grin with one of her own. "And I want to say thank you, because I know that most men would not consider my feelings as you have just done. I'm truly grateful." She reached up and touched his face then withdrew her hand quickly when she remembered their very public surroundings.

"We will have to teach you to be a bit braver with your affection," Curtis spoke, his gloved hand slowly caressing up her forearm and tracing a line back down to her wrist.

Blushing furiously, she swatted at him, earning a mischievous grin.

"Now that we've navigated the treacherous waters of my profession, I think it would be prudent to discuss our earlier topic of conversation." He laced his fingers within hers once more, his gaze shifting to their hands then back.

At her silence, he pressed further. "I assume that you were discussing a wedding date?" he asked, probing, yet surprisingly gentle.

But unfortunately, bringing back the topic that she wished to simply forget.

"Yes," Maria affirmed, meeting his gaze. "And when I expressed my hesitation to wait eight weeks till—"

"Good Lord. When I said I wasn't concerned about the date, I didn't fathom they would wait so long!" Curtis interjected.

"Eight weeks is perfectly acceptable—"

"Absolutely unacceptable. I refuse to wait that long before you're officially mine." Curtis grinned unapologetically, stroking her cheek.

Maria blushed, but continued. “I rather had the same opinion, and it was then that my mother asked if there was a *reason* for a hasty wedding.” Her face grew unbearably warm at confessing the words out loud.

“Oh.” Curtis nodded simply. “Sadly, no. There isn’t a reason. Unfortunate, that,” he added with a rakish grin.

Maria gave him a mock glare. “It was then that my mother proceeded to tell me how it simply made more sense since you… well, since you hadn’t shown any favor toward me then suddenly spoke for my hand.” Maria bit her lip.

“I see. That would appear rather sudden, should I dare look at their perspective. But I rather am exceedingly put out that your mother would think so little of your morals.” He shook his head. “Or mine. But I can understand her opinion of me. I only can apologize for the fact that my tarnished reputation has affected yours.” He gave a weak smile, shifting his attention to her hand and squeezing it tightly before releasing his grip and caressing her fingers.

“I never once thought of their opinion of you… and honestly, I do not think my mother considered that either. So be at peace, Curtis. This truly says more about them than it does you or me.” Maria waited till he glanced up. “And, in speaking about it again, I find I really couldn’t give a fig what they think.”

At this, he let out an amused chuckle. “I couldn’t agree more.”

His smile erased every trace of tension, the sensation flowing over to her as well, calming her.

“But perhaps an eight-week wait is for the best. It will halt any gossip—”

“No,” Maria interjected.

“No?”

"I refuse to wait that long. The only opinion that matters is yours. And I find that I'm quite… impatient." She gave an impertinent grin, followed by a heat surging through her at Curtis' approving and smoldering expression.

"Well, I'm sure I could talk with your father and set a date closer…"

"Or…" Maria could hardly believe she was thinking such a scandalous thought, let alone about to suggest it. "… we could escape — elope to Scotland."

"Escape? You make it sound as if we're evading arrest." He chuckled.

"In a way…" she answered with candid honesty.

He considered her for a moment, his eyes widening slowly. "You're serious?"

With a silent nod, she slowly bit her lip as anxiety returned.

His eyes darkened.

"And when would you wish to plan this… escape?" he asked, his tone melting over her like honey on a warm biscuit.

"Soon."

Curtis groaned, closing his eyes. "I don't know which is more torturous, having to wait eight weeks or having to wait even twenty-four hours, knowing that you're suggesting this option." He shook his head as if clearing it. "The temptation just might kill me."

"I do believe we have our answer then," she replied cunningly, feeling the thrill of anticipation, of victory.

"Ah, hell," he murmured in a voice so low she almost missed it. "It has to be in three days, if, *if*, this is the route we decide to take. You see, Neville and Miss Beatrix Lamont are being married by special license in two days' time. I must attend the wedding, but after…" He let the words linger.

"After… is more than suitable.

"Thursday?"

"It's my favorite day." She smiled.

"Mine too. Especially now. Good Lord, how am I going to wait for you, knowing that it's so close?" He leaned forward then glanced behind her. "Bloody chaperones."

"I rather dislike them myself. At least Lottie stays far enough away to not overhear."

"I've been watching her, just in case." He wagged his eyebrows.

"Your spy skills are most convenient."

He arched a brow. "Thank you."

"So… we're going to do this?" she asked, tightening her grip on his fingers, unwilling to let go for even a moment.

"If *you're* sure, *I* have no qualms. I've waited long enough to finally pursue you. I don't want to waste any more time."

Her heart swelled with his words, with the knowledge they revealed. And in truth, she couldn't wait to head to Gretna Green with Curtis, going home as his wife.

"Then I do believe I have some travel arrangements to get settled." He rose, extending his hand to assist with her standing as well.

"See that you do," she replied with a mischievous grin of her own, marveling in the delight of it all.

Though she was quite certain Lottie followed them back to her parents' home, she couldn't be sure. For it seemed like everything in the world had simply faded away, save herself and Curtis.

Which was exactly as it should be, when a girl was in love.

# Chapter Seventeen

TWO DAYS PASSED with the spans of eternity between, or so it seemed. When it was finally the day of the blessed nuptials of the notorious Lord Neville and the lovely Miss Beatrix Lamont, he felt as if time were moving even slower, simply to make him go mad with impatience.

The wedding was lovely, though he could be hard-pressed to remember any specific detail other than the obvious. His mind was far too preoccupied with his own plans… his own marriage.

Good Lord.

Never did he think he'd entertain such an idea, let alone be obsessed with it. But Maria? He loved her even more than he ever anticipated. Never being in love or observing it exampled in his parents and only seeing the many futile and often loveless marriages of the *ton*, he didn't quite know what to expect. So, the fullness of its power was overwhelming, glorious, utterly sinful in its all-encompassing nature.

He rather liked it.

Odd that, but the truth nonetheless.

So, as the wedding progressed, Curtis continually went over his plans. Yesterday, he had dispatched a letter under the usual guise of Rebecca Lockett to Maria, giving her the details of their *escape,* as she had so poignantly put it. He grinned to himself, delighting in the idea. This very evening, she would be waiting outside the servants' entrance to her house, dressed for travel. He warned her not to leave a note for her parents, lest they receive it too soon and give chase. Rather, he promised to dispatch a missive once they were close to Gretna Green. Even now, he had arranged his most luxurious conveyance, and with any luck, they'd simply arrive at their destination by early afternoon. It was startling, fantastic, astonishing even, to ponder how in just a day's time, he would be married. Forever tied to another, and even odder, he wasn't even the least bit hesitant.

So, as the wedding stretched into the wedding breakfast, and Neville and Beatrix made their scandalously early departure, he made his own stealthy exit. He stopped by Henry's residence, needing to take care of a few last-minute details.

"Sir?" Henry's butler gave him a once over, then grinned.

George was exceedingly odd for a butler, strangely displaying emotion. It never ceased to shock Curtis. Even now, the wide grin on the old man's face seemed extraordinarily out of place.

"Here to see the lad?" George asked, always calling Henry *lad* or *boy*, rather than the customary *sir* his name required. Of course, when one boasted at least seven decades of life, one was undoubtedly outside any requirement of social structure.

"Er, yes." He resisted the urge to add *sir* to the end of his sentences when conversing with the odd butler. "I need to deliver some instructions."

"Very good. If you'll follow me."

George led him into a simple parlor, suitable for a bachelor of only moderate means. Being the third son of a baron, Henry wouldn't be inheriting much, which was why he worked for the Crown. Curtis took a seat, watching as George quit the room, no doubt to notify Henry of his guest.

The missive felt hot in his front jacket pocket, as if it were impatient as well for its time. He withdrew the envelope and slid a gloved finger across the wax seal of his family, for once not seeing the legacy his parents had left, but the future that lay before him, a future of hope.

"Mr. Sheppard! What a surprise. To what do I owe the pleasure?" Henry asked hesitantly, as if expecting unwelcome news.

Curtis stood, offering a reassuring smile. "All is well. Kirby is still locked up and facing criminal charges. This is merely a personal call." He extended the missive and watched as Henry took it, studying the seal, reading the Moray name written on it.

"I have some news… confidential, of course."

"Of course," Henry replied automatically.

"In two days, I will give Miss Maria Garten my last name." Curtis spoke directly.

Henry blinked, swallowed, and squinted his eyes. "Pardon?"

Curtis clarified once more. "Tomorrow I eloping to Scotland, with Miss Maria Garten."

"Tomorrow," Henry repeated.

"Yes."

"I see. And this missive?" He cleared his throat and held up the letter.

"Is for my betrothed's parents. You see, there is the unfortunate circumstance where my soon–to-be wife's mother is, shall we say, being unnecessarily cruel. She has been for some time, and I wish to remove Maria from under her care as soon as possible. Maria is aware of the plan, and we hatched it together, honestly. So, we shall be making our way to Gretna Green, but in efforts to both notify — but not notify too soon — her parents of the situation, I'm leaving the missive for you to deliver, discreetly, tomorrow."

Henry nodded once. "What time, precisely?"

Curtis shifted from one foot to the other, thinking. "About four in the afternoon should be sufficient. It will give us enough of a head start so that we will not risk them catching up with us, but early enough to relieve any fears of her disappearance." He spoke the last part with a wide grin, one that Henry returned.

"I can hardly fathom. First Neville, now you? What is it in the London air? I either need to breathe deeply of it or escape completely. I'm torn as to which is the better course of action!" Henry chuckled.

Curtis closed the distance to his friend, placing a hand on his shoulder. "Breathe deeply, friend. Don't run."

"Says the man about to be taking the parson's noose willingly," Henry replied, a smile in his tone.

"Jealousy gets you nowhere, old man." With a quick nod, Curtis strode from the room.

"My congratulations. And I hope to meet this lady who has so completely stolen your senses," Henry called out, his voice causing Curtis to turn.

"Agreed. And I rather think that she gave me sense, rather than stole it." He waved, leaving.

"Congratulations, sir," George murmured as Curtis strode through the door he had just opened.

"Eavesdropper." Curtis couldn't resist goading him.

"Still hear like a boy with these ears. It's not eavesdropping if you simply happen to catch something." He shrugged unapologetically. "But I must say I'm happy for you, and tell that soon-to-be missus of yours to keep a sharp eye out for a lady for this lad." He jerked his thumb back to where Henry approached.

"None of that!" Henry waved his hands in mock terror.

Curtis shared a glance with George and nodded. Descending the steps two at a time, he strode to his waiting carriage and started home.

Only a few hours left.

A few, eternal and impatient hours.

# Chapter Eighteen

MARIA WAITED SILENTLY by the back door, the servants' entrance to her house. The air was biting, chilly with the damp moisture lingering from an earlier rain shower. Pulling her cloak about her tightly, she resisted the urge to tap a toe, instead remaining completely still, completely silent. It was her own fault; she was at least a quarter hour early, but she didn't want Curtis to wait. Rather, she wanted to see him coming and run! The past few days had passed unbearably slow. It would seem that whatever restrains her mother had exhibited before her daughter was betrothed were now dissolved, and she had taken it upon herself to cut Maria down to size, with the excuse that it was surely the only way she'd keep her husband. Perhaps it wasn't what she intended — the harsher nature — but it certainly felt that way.

As she considered her mother's words, a startling realization began to form. This wasn't a reaction to Maria; it was an action born of her own fears, of her own situation. She hadn't ever given thought to her parents' marriage. Her father was often absent, to the point of never truly seeing him but in passing. Her mother was ever-present, but rarely were they present together. Could her mother's assault on her be born of her own experience?

Maria rather thought it was, and that saddened her. It also made her exceedingly thankful that she was blessed with a love match. And of all the fears a woman could have going into marriage, she didn't fear Curtis' affection for her. In truth, she knew that over time it would only grow. He'd make a point of it, because of his own past.

The clip-clop of horse hooves pulled her from her deep thoughts, and she glanced to the street, watching as a familiar carriage rolled to a slow stop. Gasping, she took a step forward but paused. She needed to be sure.

A dark figure walked toward her, his black top hat covering his face as he bowed his head, but the stride was wonderfully familiar. As he hopped over a low stone wall, she caught sight of his face. Her entire body simultaneously melted with relief and burned with anticipation. She wanted to call out his name, but refrained, settling on meeting him halfway with her small valise in hand.

"Are you ready?" He spoke in low tones, caressing her face with his warm gaze, sending shivers of pleasure throughout her body, heating her in spite of the chilly weather.

"I've been ready for a long while," she answered.

He leaned forward, kissing her soundly. His lips were warm and intoxicating, reminding her of their day in the library, and the fact that she hadn't been able to taste his kiss since then. He pulled away far too soon, and at his gentle chuckle, she opened her eyes and arched a brow.

"All in good time. I don't want to be too distracted when we need to make haste, and you, my love, are very, devastatingly distracting." He kissed her quickly and took the valise from her grip. Then, grasping her other hand firmly in his, he walked her toward the carriage.

"Are you completely certain?" he asked, lifting her effortlessly over the small stone wall and clasping her hand once more as they took the short path to the waiting conveyance.

"Entirely."

"Brilliant. I honestly don't know what I would have done had you said anything else," he confessed with an unapologetic grin, illuminated by the silver moonlight.

"We shall never find out," she answered as he helped her alight into the carriage. As he set her valise beside her feet, he entered as well, the conveyance swaying slightly under his weight. As soon as he sat across from him, he rapped the ceiling, and the wheels lurched forward.

"How long?" Maria asked, her body quivering with excitement.

"We should be there by tomorrow evening. My carriage is very fast and well-sprung. We'll refresh the horses every few hours, and the time will fly. I've arranged for a trustworthy friend to give our news to your parents by afternoon. That will alleviate the tension, but I'm sure that they will already have their suspicions."

"Indeed. I confess, I'm not overly concerned with their reaction."

"Nor am I," Curtis replied. "Now, my love, we have a long ride ahead of us. It would be wise if you could take a moment to rest."

"Hardly." She gave a sigh of disgust. "Rest? This is the most delightful and romantic adventure I've ever imagined! I don't want to miss one moment, one second!"

Curtis' deep laugh was musical in the small carriage, filling her with even more joy. "Well, when put that way, I take back my thoughts."

"How was Neville's wedding?" Maria asked.

"Lovely, but I cannot remember any details. I'm sure it is a disappointment to you, but this I do know. It truly was a sight to see. I'm happy for the old chap. It was about time he found a wife worthy of him."

"I've heard nothing but good things about Miss Beatrix Lamont. It was truly a love match."

"Indeed. Like ours," Curtis added then reached across the carriage. He found her hand and clasped it tenderly "You're cold," he replied, his tone startled.

"A bit." Maria shrugged, pulling her hand back, not wanting him to worry about her.

"Come here." Curtis tightened his grip, not letting her fingers slip away from his, but rather pulling her toward him.

As the carriage hit a bump, she tumbled forward, and remarkably, he settled her nicely across his lap, leaving her quite confused at how she'd arrived in such a graceful fashion. "Impressive."

"You have no idea." Without another word, he captured her lips. Playfully at first, he nipped her lower one, teasing till she smiled and opened for him. It was artful, masterful how he'd slowly caressed her lower lip with his tongue, all the while gently leading her to tilt her head slightly to allow better access.

The dark of the carriage seemed to offer a curtain of privacy, one she'd never experienced before, one that made all of her inhibitions and shyness melt away as she reached up and cupped his face with her hands. His skin was soft, yet a slightly stubble caught on the fabric of her gloves as she caressed. Warmth seeped through the delicate material and heated her chilled hands. The scent of soap and peppermint mixed with some sort of spice was cloying, adding to the atmosphere as she lost herself in the millions of sensations all vying for notice within her heart, within her entire body.

He broke the kiss for a moment. "I've never tasted anything sweeter," he murmured, lowering his mouth to trail kisses along her jawline, caressing the sensitive flesh playfully as he rubbed his nose down her neck. Her breath came in soft gasps that matched the erratic beating of her heart.

"I—" She couldn't finish her thought; it was lost almost before it even began.

"I don't believe I've ever heard you speechless," Curtis remarked jokingly as he wickedly bit her earlobe before trailing kisses down her neck once more.

Rather than give a cutting reply, she simply flexed her neck to grant him better access.

"Blast this carriage," he muttered as he trailed his fingers down her shoulders, mapping the curves and igniting a passionate fire she hadn't ever imagined.

She gasped as his hands grazed her breasts, weighing them for just a moment before he groaned and moved on. Curtis clenched his hands at her waist then moved downward until finally resting them at her hips. He pulled her close, tightly against him. Heart hammering, she traced her fingers down his back, arching her fingers into his musculature and pressing her breasts into his chest, needing to feel him closer, wanting something she had no name for.

"Maria…"

Curtis groaned and met her lips once more with a searing kiss that was far less careful, less gentle than the others. It was desperate need; she recognized it because it was echoed in her own body.

Dear Lord, this is why women were ruined, because if this man pressed further, she'd willingly give in, meeting him halfway, but just as she started to slide her hands around his chest, around his coat as if to remove it, he gentled the kiss, slowly pulling away.

The first rays of sunrise were breaking through the horizon, offering a pale hue of light, just enough to see his face. His eyes smoldered with passion, and Maria almost forgot to breathe as she stared at his stunning beauty.

"Not here, love. Not only would be slightly dangerous, but your first time… I want it to be memorable because of its intensity, not its location." He gave a small chuckle, though the hunger of his expression didn't change.

"Truly?" Maria asked, leaning in and kissing him brazenly. He might be able to exercise restraint, but she wasn't. She wanted these delightful, passionate, and overwhelming sensations to never end. She tried to convey as much in the way she pursued his mouth with her own pressing into him, silently inviting.

"You'll be the death of me," he murmured against her lips, but he didn't break the embrace, just continued to kiss her. And yet, the intensity was absent, and with that, Maria slowly pulled away, her expression disappointed.

"Ha, don't fret love. I promise that you'll not have to wait long. And believe me, I shall make it entirely worth it," he promised, tapping her nose with her finger.

"See that you do," she replied coyly, earning a wicked grin in return.

"With pleasure."

# Chapter Nineteen

A JOSTLE STARTLED Curtis' musings, and he sat up straighter, listening. The coachman started to slow the horses, his loud voice calling to them as the conveyance slowed dramatically just before it gave final lurch and came to a complete halt.

"What happened?" Maria's tone was low and seductive from the slumber to which she had finally succumbed as they'd continued on their journey. Her gaze sharpened as she glanced about the carriage. It had only been a few hours, with the sun still arcing toward noon.

"I'm not entirely certain," Curtis answered, brushing a loose curl from her cheek and offering a assuring smile. "But we're perfectly safe," he finished, noticing the concerned furrow to her brow.

With a quick kiss to her hand, he reached for the door and stepped out into the chilly morning air. As he rounded the carriage, he noticed the coachman carefully studying one of the bays they'd just picked up at the last town. "What has happened?"

"Pardon, sir. But I believe he's come up lame. He refused to spring, and when he slowed, I figured we should stop before he keeled over, upsetting the carriage." The coachman turned to Curtis, his gray brows furrowed over his eyes. "'Tisn't much further to the next town, sir. What would you like to do?"

Curtis narrowed his eyes, studying the horses then turning to the carriage. This was problematic. Even if the Lord and Lady Moray didn't have the letter, they would certainly be suspicious and the risk for pursuit was great — especially if they were setting immobile on the main road. They needed to get moving, and quickly.

"Take the other bay and ride into town. Bring back another, along with a stable lad who can guide the lame horse back to the livery. I'll wait with the lady till you return." Curtis gave a swift nod and turned back to the carriage.

"Well?" Maria asked, her eyes cloudy with concern.

Curtis explained the situation as carefully as possible, noticing immediately when she caught onto the true problem.

Her eyes narrowed, her shoulders tensed, and her bow lips gave a quiet gasp. "How far are we from London?"

Curtis took a deep breath. "Several hours."

"You mean, *only* several hours," she corrected, worrying her lower lip.

"More or less."

"How long will it take for the coachman to return?" She turned her gaze to Curtis, her eyes pools of questions.

"I'm not entirely certain. We're likely halfway to the next town, and he can move faster than the carriage, so an hour, maybe two?"

"Dear Lord." She sighed. "Do you think that perhaps my parents haven't caught on?

He shrugged then reached for her hand and after reaching it, he laced his fingers through hers. "There's always a chance, love."

"I will walk to Gretna Green before I let them stop this." She spoke with a fierce intensity.

"I don't believe that will be necessary. However, this will mean that we cannot stop as often on the way," he answered, his heart pinching at the idea of her being in any discomfort. While luxurious, it was still a carriage and prone to its shortcomings.

"I do believe I'll survive," Maria replied, a weak smile teasing her lips. "Let us simply hope that this is the only hitch."

Curtis couldn't agree more.

Three hours later, Curtis wasn't as optimistic. He and Maria had talked, kissed, created a few silly games to pass the time, but now he could feel the tension crackle between them. As if punctuating the fact, rain began to pelt the roof of the carriage. Blessedly, there had been no traffic on the road, so when the clopping of horses sounded over the tapping of the rain, he was both hopeful and fearful.

"Wait here," he murmured to Maria and stepped from the conveyance. Relief flooded him when he recognized the coachman. Two horses trotted behind him with a lad astride one, likely the stable hand to attend to the lame bay.

"Whoa." The coachman pulled up before Curtis. "A thousand apologies, sir. 'Twas quite crowded. The rain started much farther north, and people are taking cover for the afternoon. I'll get these horses harnessed in right quick and send off Lynn with the lame and the one I rode to town." At Curtis' nod, he set to work.

As he stepped back into the coach, Curtis conveyed the information to Maria, who exhaled a sigh of relief as the carriage soon lurched forward.

"Thank heavens." She spoke reverently, offering him an overjoyed smile.

"Depending on the rain, we might have to stop at the next town. But if it's not too terrible, I think it best we continue on." He waited to see her response to the idea.

"Indeed," she agreed readily.

Yet, as the next town came into view, it was with relief that they stopped to rest. The rain had increased in intensity, creating quite the flood over the low road. Curtis helped Maria alight from the carriage before the Five Foxes Inn, the rain readily pelting their wool coats. The inn was veritably busting at the seams with rain-soaked travelers.

"G'day, my lord. What can I offer you and the lady?" the innkeeper asked, no doubt assessing their fine clothing and determining them worthy of his attention.

"A place to dine and freshen up," Curtis directed, yet he wondered if the innkeeper had a place to offer.

"As you can see, my lord, we're quite full. But I have one room available, and I'd be happy to bring up a private supper for you." He offered, his brown eyes gleaming with anticipation of reward.

Curtis glanced to the full room and nodded. "Indeed. Thank you." He felt Maria stiffen at his arm, and he offered her a gentle squeeze to her hand, still folded inside of his own.

In a few short moments, they led up the stairs to the room promised, the dull roar of guests fading with each step.

"Here, my lord. I'll have your supper sent up directly." With a quick nod, the innkeeper disappeared from where they'd come.

Curtis swung the door open fully, gesturing for Maria to enter. It was neat and clean, boasting one large bed and a window that displayed the muddy road they'd just traveled. "'Tis a blessing to be dry." Curtis broke the tense silence, shrugging out of his coat and setting it near the crackling fire.

"Indeed," Maria replied, her words accompanied by a delicate shiver.

"Come." Curtis opened his arms in invitation, and she willingly went to him. Her hair was damp from the rain, the scent of rosewater and lavender even more powerful as he kissed her head.

"I'm worried," she murmured against his shirt.

"'Twill be well." He kissed her head once more. "Come, let's get a bit warmer, and then we shall eat. I'm sure the rain will let up." He offered his most reassuring smile.

"Nice try." She glanced up to him, shaking her head. "I appreciate the effort though."

After dinner arrived, they partook of vegetable soup and warm crusty bread as well as a surprising array of cheeses and fruit. Curtis watched as Maria stood and walked to the window, his eyes taking in her delicate and exquisite form, curved in all the most delectable places. He rose and stood behind her, wrapping his arms around her belly and pulling her back into his chest, his body responding — reminding him that they were very alone, and there was a very available bed just behind them. Warring within himself, he deliberated silently as he traced kisses down her neck just below her ear.

She leaned into him, and he ran his nose along her skin

where her shoulder met her neck, kissing the gentle curve. At her gasp, he gently sucked the tender flesh there, savoring her flavor, the way her body responded — the way his body responded. He was just starting to turn her by her waist that he might capture her lips when she stiffened, suddenly gasping and breaking his hold.

"No," she muttered, pressing her hands against the window glass.

He followed her gaze and recognized the crest on the side of the carriage.

Moray.

"Curtis…" Maria whimpered the name, turning to face him with fear etched in her gaze.

"They can't see us up here, and my carriage is out of sight. They are simply looking. They haven't *found*." He reached up and cupped her chin gently. "We know… They do not."

"Yes. Yes, I understand." Maria blinked several times. She leaned in and kissed him gently, then pulled back. "Maybe they won't stay."

Not more than a half hour later, Curtis watched the window, and exhaled a deep sigh of relief when the carriage pulled away from the inn and disappeared down the road.

Quiet footsteps slowly approached from behind him as Maria said softly, "Are they gone?"

"Indeed. As I see it, we have two options available." He spoke quietly as he turned, finding her dainty hands. He squeezed them gently before sliding his arms around her waist, pulling her in close. "We take our sweet time and stop in Springfield rather than Gretna Green. They'll perform the ceremony just as easily."

"Or?" Maria asked, her body warm and inviting, promising that the second option would be far more enticing.

"Or we make a run for it, but it will require us to travel through the night, and in doing so, we'll surely make it to Gretna Green before they do."

Maria worried her pink lower lip, distracting him utterly. "Whoever is in pursuit — probably my father — will likely stop for the night. I think the best option is to make a run for it." She took a deep breath, then a slow smile lifted her lips, traveling to grow in her gaze.

"Then we shall do that." Curtis nodded his agreement. "I must say that was my favorite option."

"Shocking." Maria rolled her eyes playfully.

"Then I suggest we wait an hour before making our departure. We'll take a few of the lesser-traveled roads at first, and at night we'll move back to the main road, as we are less likely to come across your family."

"Brilliant. Well, I said I wanted an escape, did I not?" Maria asked, her eyes dancing with merriment.

"Ah-ha! You did! Well, you shall certainly have your escape!" Curtis chuckled, delighting in the creature that would soon be his wife, but not soon enough.

One hour.

One night.

One more day… and the whole business felt like eternity.

With the devil at their heels.

# Chapter Twenty

As they approached Gretna Green, Curtis glanced at his now-sleeping betrothed. Her lips were a perfect bow, kissable yet perfect, even in stillness. Her soft body was resting against his shoulder, her fragrance wafting around the carriage, calling to him. He'd rested but a few hours throughout the night, painfully aware of the beauty beside him, his body constantly reminding him of the fact that soon he could explore every inch of her. He forced his thoughts away, focusing on the task at hand.

In truth, they had made fantastic time. Aside from the rainstorm they'd first encountered, the weather had been blessedly clear and the horses fast. Throughout the daylight hours, he had kept a sharp eye out for the Moray conveyance but hadn't seen it. Suspicion ate at him. What if whoever was in pursuit had traveled through the night as well? He studied the approaching village with renewed scrutiny.

The small village of Gretna Green was known for its elopement availability. Just over the border into Scotland, it didn't need to follow the regulations of England and could easily perform marriages at any time, marriages that were legally binding in England. Often conducted over an anvil by a blacksmith, the ceremony wasn't necessarily a church wedding, but every bit as official. While amongst the dowagers of the *ton*, it was considered reckless and uncouth to elope in such a way, it was also known as a way to undermine the social restrictions and timelines: All in all, it was perfect for them. If there was any concern, it would be as to how the *ton* would accept Maria after eloping, but he rather thought it wouldn't be a large issue. He already had a plan in place if necessary.

As the village started to slowly pass by the carriage window, Curtis reluctantly woke his soon-to-be bride. With the softest touch, he caressed her cheek, watching in wonder as her eyes fluttered open. Confusion passed through her features a fraction of a moment before she smiled, lighting up the small space that held them. "Good morning, love," he spoke, unable to stop stroking her face, not wanting to.

Confusion crossed her features once more. "It's morning?" she asked.

Curtis chuckled. "Indeed."

"Are we there, then?" She slowly sat up and stretched her back.

His gaze greedily took in the way her curves were emphasized by the movement, his mouth growing dry and his arousal becoming more insistent. Dear Lord, he had to get a handle on this! He had to go into polite society in a few minutes.

"Yes," he answered, tearing his gaze away and looking out the window, focusing on the people milling about the street, focusing on anything but the soft mewing sound she made as she stretched again. He looked for any sign that perhaps they weren't the first ones to Gretna Green.

Marriage couldn't happen fast enough. As if providence

had heard his thoughts, they passed an inn that appeared more than suitable for their evening stay. With a deep breath and a moment of concentration on cold lakes and colder rivers, he rapped on the carriage ceiling. After a moment, his driver pulled over to the side of the cobbled road.

"I'm going to go and secure us a room. That way you can freshen up." Without waiting for a reply, he gave her a quick kiss and stepped from the carriage. He gave a quick word to the coachman, who maneuvered the carriage so that it was partly hidden behind a large cart on the side of the road. It wasn't a perfect hiding place, but it would have to do.

With no trouble at all, he secured the finest room. He made sure to tell the innkeeper that his *bride* accompanied him, so that there would be no talk, but it would be prudent for them to take care of that detail as soon as possible, especially with time being precious.

As he returned to take Maria up to their room, his gaze scanned the street for an anvil sign. Upon seeing one, he made a mental note and helped his betrothed gently down from the carriage.

The room was plain but clean, and, as mercy would have it, a large bed dominated the space. Curtis couldn't help the smile that spread across his face.

"This is lovely," Maria said, walking to the window, a faint blush tinting her cheeks as she glanced to the bed and back to the window's view.

"Indeed." Curtis cleared his throat, focusing on the task at hand. "I'm going to leave you with your valise to take a moment for yourself. I'll be back shortly, but I need to secure our blacksmith," he finished with a wink, earning another blush. How he loved her innocence mixed with a bit of seductress that made an appearance in the carriage ride.

"See that you hurry," she replied.

Oh, how he hoped the tension in her voice was due to anticipation, rather than worry.

"Yes, my lady." With a bow, he crossed the distance of the room and kissed her soundly, not lingering too long lest he be tempted to test the bed prematurely, and left without a backward glance.

Securing a blacksmith to perform the ceremony wasn't difficult at all; rather, it was deciding which *one* that proved difficult. But settling on the smith closest to the inn, he paid the fee and promised to return shortly with his bride-to-be.

Maria was waiting eagerly for him when he opened the door to the room, and he could see that she had readjusted her dress and fixed her slightly mussed hair. The sunlight pouring through the window created a glow about her that stole his breath, and the effect was compounded by her smile, only for him.

"Are you ready?" he asked when he found the voice to speak.

"Impatient, actually," she replied, a look of utter mischief in her gaze that set his blood to boiling.

"Then I shall not keep my lady waiting." He bowed crisply and then extended his hand. She accepted his hand, and despite her words, he could feel a slight tremble in her touch.

"Are you sure?" he whispered as they took the stairs slowly.

"About you? Yes. I'm just a bit nervous. Never been married before, you know." She winked, but her smile was slightly anxious.

"Neither have I," he replied, earning a more relaxed grin.

She laughed gently as they exited the inn, the bustle of

the small town pulling them in as they wound around a parked cart and nodded to other people they passed. In short time, they arrived at the blacksmith, and Curtis opened the wooden door, giving his eyes a moment to adjust to the dimly lit room. Smoke peppered the air, along with the dry heat of the forge.

"Aye, are you ready, then?" the burly blacksmith asked in his thick brogue. He set down a metal rod, its end glowing red, and took off his thick leather gloves. With a bright white smile in strict contrast to the smudges of soot on his face, he welcomed them.

"Yes. Let me introduce you to my soon-to-be-wife, Miss Maria." He left off the last name, just at the happenstance that the old Scotsman would recognize the Garten name, it being Scottish as well.

"Aye, a lovely lass indeed. Shall we begin?" he asked, nodding once and striding to an anvil that was far cleaner than the other.

Curtis glanced to Maria, who offered a rueful grin as she walked to the anvil, still holding his arm.

"Are you in agreement with this marriage, miss?" the blacksmith asked, his gaze somber as he regarded Maria carefully.

"Indeed." She nodded firmly.

"Verra well." He cleared his throat. "Let me fetch my wife and her friend, to serve as witnesses. 'Tis important that I make sure the lass is willin' before I go any further, you understand."

Curtis nodded sagely and watched as the large man disappeared further into the blacksmith's shop and returned shortly with two women.

"Now then. Place your hands here over the anvil.

Curtis gave a quick reassuring smile to Maria, noticing her hand still trembled slightly, and rested their intertwined hands over the cold metal.

"Do ye pledge yer troth to love this women fer yer whole life, in health, in sickness, in poverty, or riches?" he asked Curtis with a tone of levity.

"I do pledge my troth," Curtis replied, his tenor strong like the conviction of his heart. He glanced to Maria, willing her to feel the same conviction, the same certainty as he felt about her.

"Lass, do you pledge yer troth to love this man yer whole life, in health, in sickness, or poverty, or riches?" he asked.

"I do, indeed," she replied, her tone musical, strong and assured. A smile broke across his lips as he met her gaze, memorizing the moment.

"Then I declare before God and these here witnesses that, by your words, yer entered in holy marriage. Amen." He gave a quick nod and then winked. "Ye can kiss yer bride if ye wish now, lad."

Curtis laughed and turned, pulling Maria in close and rejoiced as she met him halfway, kissing him unabashedly, without restraint. He could taste her joy, simply an echo of his own.

"Aye, laddie, save some for later." The black smith chuckled.

Curtis broke the kiss first, loving that already this was a pattern. Never had she simply pulled away from him; it had always been he restraining her. What a glorious promise for things to come!

"Now be off with ye, and have a blessed union." The blacksmith grinned again and turned back to his forge, the women giving their own smiles of approval and then disappearing in the back from where they'd come.

"Well, Mrs. Sheppard," Curtis said her name in a low voice, reverently, yet with unrestrained joy.

"Mr. Sheppard," Maria replied, though she bit her lip.

He reached up and caressed her cheek, marveling in the moment. "We made it." He bent down and gave a joyful kiss to her lips.

He felt her mouth stretch into a smile even as he continued to kiss her, then she pulled slightly away.

"And here I thought there was more to the marriage."

And with a wink, she led the way to the inn, taking his heart with her.

# Chapter Twenty-One

**H**USBAND. WIFE. MARIA kept thinking the words over and over, grinning to herself at the knowledge of it all. Not simply because she was now married, but because of whom she had married. Her grin widened as she watched his knee bob impatiently while they waited for the last of their dishes to be removed from dinner. He was trying so hard to be patient, to do what was best for her.

And finally, it was time to be altogether finished with waiting.

For both of them.

"Finally," he breathed, only low enough for her to hear, but anyone watching his expression would have gathered the same meaning. His countenance was impatient and passionate, relieved and exasperated. A giggle escaped her lips at the sight of it.

He squeezed her elbow gently. Even with the dull roar of the other patrons of the inn, it was as if the world closed in on simply the two of them. And as they left it all behind and ascended the stairs, every aspect of creation faded away, save Curtis.

Her husband.

Silently, he opened the door to their room, and immediately her eyes took in the bed. How was it that it seemed larger, slightly more intimidating? She was ready for this — more than ready — yet to be so vulnerable was unnerving.

And innocent. Dear Lord, she was innocent, and Curtis was… well…

Not.

A cold sweat broke out across her flesh as insecurities she never had pondered before came leaping to the forefront of her mind, and suddenly she wasn't as ready as she'd thought.

What if…

What if she wasn't good at it?

What if she disappointed him?

What if—

"Maria?" Curtis' gentle voice pulled her back from the edge of panic. "Are you well, love? You've turned quite pale." His hands reached up and slowly framed her face, his warm touch soothing her somewhat.

"I— It's just…" She swallowed, taking a deep breath.

"Tell me. Please. Are you afraid? I promise—"

"No — yes — I mean… what if I'm not… pleasing?" Her body flushed with the humiliation of her words. Yet, hadn't Curtis told her that he valued honesty above all things? Could she honestly trust him with this and walk away unscathed?

He chuckled gently, the sound causing her heart to stall then pick up its pace. Why would he laugh?

"Love, it is utterly impossible for you to not please me," he said, slowly tracing his hands down her neck, across her shoulders with a feather-like caress, and then resting at her hips. He tugged her toward him, each step guiding her into his arms.

"Are you sure?" she asked, willingly relaxing into his embrace, soaking in his inviting warmth.

"Certain," he murmured and kissed the top of her head, melting more of her fear away like ice on a spring day.

"How can you be so sure?" she asked, the final remnants of her insecurity having a voice.

"Because I've never loved anyone like I love you. You're it, and you alone have my heart, my name, everything." Curtis whispered the words against her hair. He released one hand on her hip and started to pull out the pins of her hair, allowing the locks to fall from their place to flowing along her back. His other hand lightened his hold on her and helped, and all while she listened to the way his heartbeat leapt with an increasing rhythm as he finished.

"So, utterly beautiful," he vowed.

Warm hands guided her from the secure place at his chest, and as she lifted her gaze to meet his, the last of her insecurities evaporated.

"You can't imagine how many times I dreamed of this," he confided, lifting a lock of hair and rubbing it in his fingers. A moment later, he wrapped his arms around her once more and captured her lips in a scorching kiss. His lips tasted hers, nipping and playing, and performing the dance of give and take.

She pressed into him, owning his kiss, returning it, loving him with every brush of her tongue against his, with every tilt of her head, every breath that she took.

Now bold, she felt the delight and anticipation of earlier, when they were locked in passion in the carriage. All inhibitions scattered as she slid her arms up his chest, noticing the tone of his stomach through his shirt as she guided him in taking off his coat. The offending garment hit the ground, making a soft thud, and immediately she started to untuck his shirt, allowing her greedy hands to slip up his back and caress the bare flesh. He groaned against her lips as she pressed in harder, his state of arousal leaving little to the imagination.

Appearing not to be outdone, Curtis deftly began unbuttoning her gown, all while trailing kisses down her neck, a few times muttering an impatient curse that only made her smile. At those times, she'd taken the opportunity to tug on his hair or bite his lip, something to distract him even further. At which he'd mumbled, "minx" and taken her lips in a delightfully sinful kiss.

Her hands made short work of his dress shirt buttons and removed the remaining garments from his chest. She broke the kiss just long enough to take in the view, last of which was a knowing smirk from her husband.

"I utterly approve," she affirmed, taking his lips once more.

As he finally finished her buttons, he released her from his kiss, and with a gloriously passionate gaze, he slowly slid the dress from one shoulder then the other, allowing her to remove her arms before the fabric pooled at her feet. Though still in her undergarments, she felt entirely naked as his eyes accounted for every inch, every curve, as if studying and marveling at a masterpiece. "You're utterly glorious… and still very clothed." He lifted the edge of her chemise. As the garment was slowly removed, the cool air caused gooseflesh to rise on her skin. His gaze greedily took her in. "Lovely, so breathtakingly lovely."

She trembled from the vulnerability of it all as he slowly removed the last of her clothing, till nothing veiled her.

Chilled and tense with anticipation, she watched as he met her gaze. He discarded his breeches in a quiet heap, pausing for just a moment before reaching out to her, his hand extended as he shared her vulnerability.

Gave her a choice to share his.

One quiet step at a time, Maria joined him, and his body heated, immediately calling to her as she wrapped her arms around his neck. She met his gentle kiss, warming to it as it built, as it grew…

From mere warmth to scorching fire.

She didn't feel the cold any longer; rather, a heat from the inside surged through her, demanding more, needing more. Curtis must had felt the same hunger for he lifted her into his arms and strode toward the bed, kissing her deeply with each step till he slowly laid her on the bed. He covered her at once with his scorching heat, pressing into her, but not completely.

Not yet.

She wound her legs around his, arching her back as he nipped her neck, her fingers curving into his musculature, into his broad shoulders and the hills and valleys of his back.

"Are you ready for me?" he asked, clearly not expecting a response as he captured her lips once more, stealing her chance to avow, and in return, her body simply sang the affirmation as she arched into him once more.

Maria's body tensed as he slowly completed her, expecting pain, expecting something other than the blissful, unimaginable pleasure that followed. And as he moved, the world began to shift, shatter, and in expectation, even her heartbeat seemed to follow the same splendid disarray of passion till everything in her world exploded, causing her to cry out and gasp for air. Slowly she awakened from the brilliant sensations, only to careen over the edge once more as Curtis found his own release.

As her heartbeat slackened, matching itself to the one echoed just above her own, she kissed his shoulder, breathing deeply the wonder of it all.

Curtis lifted himself on his elbow, his expression full of adoration. "I love you," he vowed just before kissing her slightly swollen lips.

"I love you more," she murmured against his own, then kissed him again.

"Doubtful."

"Watch me."

"Shhh…" he said against her shoulder.

"Never."

"I know."

She narrowed her eyes, even as her body trembled from his touch.

"And I wouldn't have it any other way."

With that, he kissed her into silence, restarting everything they had just explored.

# Epilogue

"For the love of all that is holy, would you please not touch him?" Curtis whispered quietly, not wanting his beloved wife to wake their son, Jonathan Ansley Sheppard.

Again.

Because each night, she'd pressed a hand to his soft golden curls, kissed his soft hand, and as she walked away, he'd wake.

And, of course, that meant that she was picking him up, cuddling him — as any mother should. But this evening, Curtis was rather impatient for his wife. It was their anniversary, and as such, he was determined to have her completely to himself.

In his bed.

Their bed.

As Maria gave him a rueful glare, she simply bent down and blew a kiss to their cherubic son and then slowly left, placing her soft and warm hand within his own.

As they closed the door gently, Curtis felt his entire body relax.

Miracles did happen.

"Can you imagine it's been a year?" Maria asked,

squeezing his hand as they walked toward their bedchamber.

"Yes. There's been quite a bit of life packed into these past months." He offered her a grin.

"At least your parents have finally forgiven us."

"You can thank your son for that," Maria badgered.

Upon returning to London, they'd discovered that it was indeed her father who had pursued them, but he'd arrived a day late. As a result, Lord and Lady Moray had all but refused to see them, unless forced upon in polite society. It had been surprisingly ineffectual as punishments went. The estrangement had given them the freedom to grow together as man and wife, rather than feel the necessity to include family in their affairs. It had been a learning experience for both of them, especially when Maria proved very ill just about six weeks after the wedding. It was Lady Langley that had to offer some insight as to why Maria couldn't keep food down.

A baby.

And the chink in Lord and Lady's armor, as it were.

Soon all was forgiven — if not forgotten — at the sight of little Jonathan. And while they were not on entirely friendly terms, Jonathan would grow up knowing the affection of a doting grandmother and grandfather.

And together with Maria, he had quite discovered that being a family was the most adventurous, dangerous, and delightful experience one could ever have. Dangerous because of the fragility of a newborn and well, even at two months, the child was already proving to be into mischief, something his wife blamed entirely on him.

He couldn't exactly argue the point.

And an adventure, because he could never really anticipate what would happen next. Life was blissfully happy, and he was going to see that the joy it brought continued far into this night.

"I love you." Maria's voice called him from his musings, and he turned, kissing her soundly.

"Not nearly as much as I love you," he spoke against her lips, as was their usual argument.

"I—"

"Now, no more talking. I haven't had my fill of you yet, so I'll have to silence you the only way I know how." He gave a firm nod and swept his wife into his arms then closed the distance to their bedchamber, softly shutting the door behind them.

"Oh?" Maria asked, her eyes glinting with that same mischievous gleam, the one that still sent his blood to surging, his body to responding with absolute attention. "And here I thought you were going to write me a letter," she teased.

"Letters are long over," he muttered against her lips. "Letters are vastly overrated when I can simply kiss you instead."

"Letters worked, my love," Maria reminded him, her hand caressing his jawline as she kissed his lips.

"I'm still amazed to this day about that fact." He only paused the kiss briefly to speak.

"It is, after all, how you silence a rogue," she answered, giggling against his lips.

His grin widened as he laid her on their bed. "Ah, but you forget, I know how to silence *you.*"

"Oh?"

"Indeed." And without further delay, he kissed his life companion, otherwise occupying her lips, as well as the rest of her, far into the night.

Silencing her in the only way he knew, in the only way he'd ever wish her to keep silent.

By speaking love through a kiss.

Don't miss Neville and Beatrix story in "A Tempting Ruin," Book 3 of the GreenFord Waters Series. Available Now!

**A Tempting Ruin**
**Kristin Vayden**

# PROLOGUE

At first, she thought she was alone.

To be honest, at first she was… sitting in front of the fire in a rather comfortable chaise and immersing herself in a fantastic book.

Then the door opened and closed so quietly she almost didn't glance up from her page.

However, as providence would have it, she did indeed glance up and saw a gentleman enter and stride purposefully toward the window overlooking the back wood.

She should have spoken up, for it was forbidden to be in a room alone with an available gentleman, but she couldn't find the moral power to open her mouth. Rather, she simply watched him.

His olive-green jacket accentuated his shoulders, and the tan breeches highlighted the contour of his muscular legs.

He was glorious, with raven-black hair cut shorter than the common style, but it fit his angular jawline — or what she could see of it. The rest she imagined, knowing his face, having seen him before, but it was unlikely that he could boast the same recognition of her.

"Are you quite done?" he asked, causing a painful blush to heat her face as she realized he was aware of her study of his person.

However, feeling a bit of her hoyden streak, she simply replied, "No, if you'll please shift to the side..."

His slow turn as he shifted to face her gave a view of his amused expression as he held out his hands, proving his amicability to her request.

"Is this better?"

"Indeed. Though I must ask why you felt it necessary to hide in the library," Beatrix asked, setting her book aside and straightening her posture.

"I aim to please." He nodded then took a few lazy steps toward her. "I'm not hiding... I'm simply... enjoying some peace."

"In a room you thought to be empty?"

"What if I told you I knew it wouldn't be empty?"

"Then I'd say that I'm no fool... easily led to believe a lie," she shot back. "I have sisters, you know."

"Indeed… Miss Beatrix." He bowed then raised a daring eyebrow.

"Hmm… either we've been introduced, and I've already forgotten your person — which isn't a recommendation — or you're exceedingly forward."

"Says the lady that just asked me to turn for her visual benefit."

"True…" Beatrix shrugged. "…though I am curious how you know my name, Lord Neville."

"Ah, so I am not unknown. You are indeed a minx, are you not?" he teased.

Beatrix studied him. This was likely the oddest conversation she'd ever have in her life… completely against the rules of Society. Yet it was entirely diverting!

"Perhaps."

"Ah, keep your secrets then." He shrugged and approached her, glancing at her book. "Enjoying it?"

"I was…" Beatrix let the words linger.

"You wound me. Is my sparkling conversation not enough to satisfy your need for amusement?"

"No." She shrugged and picked up her book. She studied the page for a moment while watching him from the corner of her eye.

His grin broke through, giving her an unfocused view of his white teeth.

"It's working, you know." He spoke as he moved to sit in the wingback chair across from her.

"What is working?" she asked dryly, continuing to study the page.

"Graham is practically going mad."

At this, Beatrix glanced up, feeling her brow furrow. "I'm sure I don't understand what you mean." How was it possible that he had caught on to their ploy? In truth, the whole house party was simply a strategy to get Lord Graham to finally offer for her sister, helped along by the implication that Lord Neville was pressing his suit for Bethanny's hand as well, even if he wasn't. But *he* wasn't supposed to know it wasn't true! Neither of them!

"Do not pretend with me. Anyone with half the sense of a toad can discern your stratagem. I was just letting you know it was indeed successful. I must admit that adding my involvement was a nice touch. Though I'd never actually offer for Miss Lamont, I could have put on quite the show." He shook his head.

"Who are you?" Beatrix felt the need to ask. How was it possible he knew so much about their private endeavors?

"Edwin Rowland, Eighth Earl of Neville, my lady." He gave a jaunty nod of his chin.

She studied him then tentatively offered her own name. "Beatrix Lamont — Miss Lamont to you."

"A lovely name, I say."

"Thank you."

The silence lingered for a few moments, but it wasn't uncomfortable, rather a peaceful lull.

Beatrix lifted her book once more.

"What is it you are reading?"

"Ah, I doubt you'd approve." She shot him a glance over the page.

"Try me."

*"Lady Maybelle's Mysterious Suitor."*

"It's the butler." He leaned forward and grinned evilly.

"What? No. You did not… I—" Beatrix stood, closed the book, and paced irritated. Opening the book, she glanced to the last page and read, her fury rising by the moment.

"It *was* the butler! You ruined it!" she all but shouted as she lifted the book. For a fleeting moment, she wanted to throw it at him! How dare he ruin the fantastic book, the sweet mystery, by giving away the ending! Of all her pet peeves, this was champion.

"I do hope you're a poor aim if you decide to follow through with hurling the volume at my head." He stood and held up his hands.

"Why? Why would you *do* that?" Beatrix lamented, tossing the book on the chaise and glaring at him.

"Because it amuses me."

She stilled, knowing her glare grew more menacing by the moment as she studied the horrible creature she had, only moments ago, thought so devastatingly attractive. "It… amuses you?"

"Rather, *you* amuse me. Your reaction." He lifted his shoulder in a blasé manner, as if he hadn't just provoked her!

"I — you — you!" Beatrix ground out then stomped.

"Did you just stomp?" he asked, his grin growing.

"A lady doesn't stomp. There was a spider," she lied and stalked away toward the window, hoping the horrible man would get the point and take his leave.

The sound of footsteps approaching had her stiffening her back.

"I'm sorry for offending you so greatly. But I do thank you for being the cause of such a prized few moments of amusement. It was… delightful. And I'll tell you a secret…" His voice was close, sending prickles of awareness up her arms as his velvet voice spoke softly.

"Humbled to be your entertainment, sir," she replied

frostily, trying to keep her reaction to him hidden away and forgotten. After turning to face him, she shifted her gaze from him to the door meaningfully.

His amused chuckle was the only response.

*Drat.*

"If you read the next book, you'll find out a little bit more about the butler… because, Miss Beatrix, things are not what they always seem," he replied kindly and then turned to leave.

"Wait," she called out before she'd thought about it.

He paused and turned to her, his gray eyes clear and completely drawing her in.

"You don't have to leave just yet."

"I do believe that is the kindest thing you've said to me." He bit back a grin.

Barely resisting the urge to roll her eyes, Beatrix walked over to the bookshelf where she had originally found the book and looked for the sequel. "What is the title of the second book?" she called over her shoulder.

Lord Neville smiled and glanced down, then strode toward her. *"The Butler's Secret."*

"Oh! I can't wait." She smiled as she searched. "Ah! There it is!" She stood on her very tiptoes, reaching for the book, her fingers brushing the spine and missing in the effort to withdraw it.

"Blast it all," she mumbled.

"Such language from a lady!" Lord Neville scolded, tsking his tongue.

In spite of his grin, which bespoke his unoffended nature, Beatrix still felt her face heat with a painful blush.

"Allow me."

"No, I've got it." She tried again.

"Very well." Lord Neville stepped back, crossing his arms.

After several additional attempts to dislodge the book, Beatrix sighed and turned to face him. "Can you please help?"

"I thought you'd never ask, though I must say the… stretching… offered a very pleasant view of your ankles," he replied as he brushed past her and began to reach for the book.

"Ooo…" Beatrix elbowed him in the ribs just as he stretched.

"What the—" He dislodged the book only slightly and turned to glare at her. "Was that necessary?"

"You were looking at my ankles," she replied haughtily.

"You were looking at *me* earlier." He crossed his arms, knowing he had won the argument, judging by the triumphant gleam in his eyes.

"The book, please?" Beatrix shifted the topic of conversation.

"Here." He easily reached the book's spine and removed it to the point of where it was teetering on the edge.

"You simply could not resist, could you?" Beatrix grumbled as she reached and pulled out the book.

"No," he answered honestly, "but to be honest… if you were in my position, would you have done any different?"

"No… wait. Yes."

He cocked his head, waiting.

"I would have tried to make the book fall on your head," Beatrix replied then dashed across the room.

"Unbelievable!" he called out and gave chase.

"You're simply jealous I thought of it rather than you." She spoke as she strategically stepped, placing the chaise between them.

"I'd never do anything so diabolical to a lady," he shot back then slowly circled the chaise.

Beatrix matched him step for step till they'd made a full lap around the piece of furniture.

"This is pointless," he replied, walked away, and sat in the chair. He reached for a book on the side table and began reading.

Beatrix watched him for a moment then took a seat as well.

Halfway into the first chapter of her book she glanced up, noticing that Lord Neville was not across from her any longer.

"Lesson one… never let your guard down," he whispered from beside her.

"How did you do that?" she asked, startled that she had missed his movement.

"Shouldn't you be more concerned with why?" he asked.

Beatrix swallowed, trying not to notice how his nearness radiated comforting warmth or how the very air was permeated with a masculine spicy scent that called to her. "Why?"

"In this case… it was the only way I could get close enough to do this," he whispered as he leaned in slightly. His hand reached up and gently placed a lock of hair behind her ear.

"What if… if I don't want you to?" Beatrix asked, knowing full well how much she *did* want him too; however, the last thing she wanted was for him to know that!

"Then simply say no," he murmured, his gaze darting

from her lips to her eyes once more. "Are you… going to say no?"

Beatrix blinked, unable to break the swirling fog of desire that wound around them like mist from the sea. "No."

He leaned away, and Beatrix realized the misunderstanding. He had thought she'd meant she didn't welcome his affection!

Quickly, she reached up and placed her hand against his cheek, immediately feeling his warm skin through her glove.

Hope dawned in his expression, and immediately he closed the distance and pressed his mouth to hers, caressing them softly.

Longingly.

He withdrew slightly, but only to tilt his head further before placing another kiss to her lips, sliding his across hers softly, invitingly. She reached up and placed her hand at his shoulder, pulling him in closer, a request he immediately obeyed. His kiss deepened, and Beatrix lost herself in the thousands of blissful sensations that were all awakening each moment. She almost gasped when his velvet tongue slid across her lower lip a second before his teeth playfully nipped at it.

Not wanting to be outdone, she tentatively mimicked his actions, glorying in his reaction as her hand at his shoulder felt the telling bunching of his musculature as he leaned in deeper to their shared kiss. With each nip and caress, she gave and took, a constant partner in the dance, moving with the music of desire awakening.

The sound of voices, angry voices, interrupted Beatrix's blissful state and shook her back to the reality of her situation.

She was alone.

With an unmarried gentleman.

Which was enough to consider her compromised, not to mention she had been willingly participating in a far-more-than-chaste kiss.

Heaven's above, Carlotta would have her hide!

As if sensing her thoughts, Neville withdrew. His stormy grey gaze searched her face, memorizing her. "I'm… I shouldn't have." He glanced away, as a cold chill hit her chest. "You are fascinating in a way that is dangerous, Miss Beatrix, and, for that reason, I must leave. Regardless of how… right now… I very much want to stay."

What did one say to that? For that matter, what did one say after a kiss? Speechless, Beatrix nodded, confused.

However, as the voices grew louder, Lord Neville stood and straightened his jacket then strode to the door.

Beatrix only saw him one other time before he quit the house party they were attending.

Then all thought of stolen kisses and ruined novels faded into the background when the duke received a cryptic threat against her. Though orphaned, she and her sisters, Berty and Bethanny, were staggeringly wealthy, not to mention the wards of the Duke of Clairmont. With Bethanny safely married to Lord Graham and Berty still quite young, Beatrix had been left with the target at her back, or so the officer from Scotland Yard had said to the duke.

It had been less than two weeks since the house party, but it felt like several years. At first, the duke had been told that the death of her parents had not been accidental. Yet, as horrific as such a claim had been, it hadn't added up.

Within a few days, another officer had informed them of new evidence that suggested it was a false lead. The only tangible information they could disclose was that Beatrix was a target for *something*.

Helpful.

Each time an officer would come to the door, Beatrix would find herself holding her breath, wondering, fearing.

Enough was enough. So when the duke devised a plan to remove her from the public eye, just to be cautious, she'd agreed. Anything would be better than simply living in fear. No one could know where she traveled. To cover their plan, the duke would claim she'd been taken, kidnapped.

Beatrix thought the whole ordeal overly dramatic, but what could one do?

So she'd played along, hoping everything would conclude quickly. And, in the meantime, she'd dream about stolen kisses, and try to forget about an evil that lurked in the London shadows.

# CHAPTER ONE

*A year later*

EDWIN ROWLAND, EIGHTH Earl of Neville, flexed his hands as he gripped the bannister overlooking the small garden of the inn that housed him for the night. The song of the crickets did nothing for his taut nerves. Paradoxically, his heart pounded with a fierce dread and anticipation. There was no sign of her.

It was as if she had vanished. Of their own accord, his fingers bit into the stone railing, grasping for control of something.

Lord only knew how much he needed control right then.

Of anything.

The sun had long set, and the stars twinkled in the ink sky, yet he didn't notice their beauty, only forced his thoughts from the woman he couldn't forget.

A woman he had not known nearly long enough to create such an… attachment.

But that didn't make it less real.

Her ebony hair beckoned for his touch; rather, he burned to test the weight of the unbound tresses. Eyes the color of warm caramel and a smile that was equal parts sass and intelligence haunted him.

And as quick as he'd found her…

She'd been taken.

Life was too ironic. The unwelcome sensation of déjà vu tickled his mind, yet he repressed it.

He'd not think of that now. No, now he needed to focus, to think. Harboring himself in the Fox Inn, he was grasping at straws.

But he had promised, to a duke no less.

And with his experience with the War Office, he was truly the best man for the job. London held no lure anyway, not when he knew the price paid to withhold the truth, and when only judgment and a reclusive life waited for him.

As he searched for Beatrix, Miss Lamont, he reminded himself, it was as if life held more purpose, more value. It was a bright temptation to hope once more.

Yet with each day that passed with no sign of her, the bleak realization poured over him anew.

Yet, he'd given his word, and he'd not fail.

He would find her.

"YOU, THERE!" LORD Neville strode toward the stable boy, taking in his smudged face along with the wary look that lit his gaze.

"Aye, gov'ner." The lad nodded, his blue eyes narrowing in a mix of fear and respect.

"Could you tell me who that horse belongs to?"

He nodded to the black mare; her highly arched neck and impatient paw at the ground further affirmed his suspicions. She was a beauty, horseflesh of quality, of money. It was a rarity for gentry to be abiding in such a small inn during the season. Any, *any,* oddity, anything that seemed out of place begged his attention.

"Tha' one? Ach, she's a beauty, sir. A grand lady had ta leave her here, tossed a shoe and came up lame. The stable master, he fixed her up real nice, but the lady left before she was ready to ride. Bought a horse in town, she did."

Lord Neville nodded and turned to the horse. The mare's ears pricked and twisted as she snorted and seemed to wait for his next move. "What did the lady look like?" he asked, keeping his tone slightly disinterested.

"Well… she was a fine one. Fancy dress and all. Smiled too. Had a right pretty girl with her, tho' I suppose 'twas a lady too, the way she spoke and dressed."

"Hmm…" Lord Neville replied, pacing back to the lad. "What did the younger lady look like?" He bent down to the lad's level, watching him.

"Right pretty, sir. Brown hair all tied up like ladies do, and a fine dress like the older lady. They seemed quite happy to be together."

"I see." Lord Neville stood, no longer feeling that he might be onto the trail of the missing woman. He steeled himself as he thought her name: Beatrix.

"Oh! I almost forgot, sir. The older lady, she left this." The stable boy spun and ran to a tack room and disappeared. In a moment, he returned with a small square of linen.

He reached out and accepted it from the stable boy. The trim around the edges was feminine, delicate. But it was the initials embroidered into the corner that confused him.

*SR*

Keeping his face impassive, he folded the linen and stuffed it into his greatcoat pocket. "Thanks, lad." He withdrew a coin and tossed it to the boy, who caught it midair and grinned.

"Thank you!" He scrambled off, clutching the coin tightly in his fist.

The dark horse nickered behind him, and Lord Neville glanced behind him, narrowing his eyes and studying the animal once more. A suspicion crept along his mind, and he turned, leaving the hay-rich stable behind and choosing to cross the worn dirt street.

The Fox Chase Tavern was only a moment's walk, and in little time, he entered the dimly lit establishment. The air was thick with the scent of spilled ale and earthy humanity. Once his eyes adjusted, he took a seat near the bar keep, signaling for an ale.

After taking a sip of the stout brew, he waved at the tender.

The portly gentleman ambled over to him, a slight limp to his stride. He leaned up on the bar and raised his bushy white eyebrows. "Aye?"

"My aunt has a cottage around these parts, but my coachman is ill, and I'm needing to find her residence on my own. Could you please direct me to the estate of Lady Southridge?" Lord Neville kept his gaze open, knowing he was taking a long shot in the dark.

"Southridge, eh? Well, ye aren't too far from it. If ye take Kippen Road out of town, you'll follow it till ye hit the tree line, walnut trees, I believe. Past that is the gate to Breckridge House." He nodded once and stood straight.

After wiping his hands on a towel at the bar, he left to attend another patron.

*Southbridge.*

What in the hell was he supposed to do with that information? Of course he was going to pay a visit to the Lady Southridge at her estate, but would Beatrix be there?

Safe and sound?

*Not* kidnapped?

Simply… taken without informing anyone?

Though Lord Neville wasn't too familiar with Lady Southridge, the rumors of her unorthodox behavior made him accept the possibility that this, indeed, was possibly the case in Beatrix's situation.

But what then?

Dear heavens above, he had to tell the duke.

The duke who viewed Lady Southridge as a maternal figure.

Could the day get worse?

Bloody betraying lot, all of them! This was why he avoided London, the whole season of the misbegotten *ton*.

It was a nightmare — a pox on them all!

Regardless, he was under obligation to ferret out the truth. He had promised.

And he never went back on his word.

Ever.

"ISN'T THE SUNSHINE lovely?" Beatrix Lamont fanned herself slightly with her white-gloved hand as she walked along the stone path toward the orangery.

"There's nothing sweeter than sunshine after such miserable rain," Lady Southridge affirmed, her green eyes crinkling as she gave Beatrix a warm smile.

Beatrix inhaled deeply, thankful for the fresh and crisp air of the English countryside. It was a stark contrast to the stench and smoke-hazed air of London. After all, she and her sisters had been raised near Bath, close enough to the sea that the slight flavor of salt lingered in the air.

A lingering fear clenched in her heart as she momentarily thought over the reasons for her exile from London. As stagnant as the air was in town, it was still, in a way, home. It was there she'd found a new place to belong with her guardian, the Duke of Clairmont and his wife, Carlotta. Pushing those thoughts aside, she let her gaze linger on the gardens of Breckridge House. It was a pleasure to enjoy the soft incline of the hills and the smattering of trees that lined the long drive. Not a horizon filled with stone buildings, but pure nature.

"It's a beautiful view, is it not?" Lady Southridge's voice pulled her from the abandon of the scenery.

"Indeed," Beatrix murmured.

"And you're safe here, Beatrix. You're safe." Lady Southridge's tone took on a protective edge, a fierceness that was familiar, yet foreign. For, while the older woman was indeed fierce, it was usually in some misbegotten meddling scheme… nothing quite as serious as protecting Beatrix's very life.

"I know." Beatrix sucked in a tight breath, not willing to dwell on the what ifs that plagued her at night…

But failing to keep her imagination in check.

"No one knows… rather… no one that needs to know

knows… if that makes sense."

Beatrix glanced to her, watching as a confused expression darkened her green eyes before she waved her hand. "But I do apologize for the need for your disguise… it goes against the grain for me to set you up as a bluestocking in the house." She shook her head slightly, her silvering reddish hair not moving from its perfect design under her straw bonnet.

"I understand. Besides, a lady's companion isn't exactly arduous work." Beatrix shook her head in amusement.

"Well… you've not been in my employ for long," Lady Southridge shot back, grinning.

"True. Yet, I find I'm unable to summon the proper amount of trepidation for my position," Beatrix quipped.

"Such cheek! Don't you know you cannot speak to your betters in such a way?" Lady Southridge feigned insult a moment before a grin broke through her attempt at a stern glare.

"Yes, ma'am. A thousand apologies," Beatrix murmured, bowing a curtsy and averting her gaze.

Lady Southridge's snort broke through her facade of humility, and she grinned in spite of herself.

"You do that, and I'll set you up as a scullery maid," the older woman threatened.

Beatrix glanced up to her annoyed expression. Her lips were pressed together tightly, as if trying to hold back laughter.

Her hypothesis was proven true when Lady Southridge glanced away, chuckling. "I do give you credit for your acting abilities, my dear."

"Thank you." Beatrix took a moment to bow.

"That being said, I've not told a soul in the house's

employ the truth of the situation. As far as they are all concerned, you are Beverly Blithe, my companion. I breeched conduct when I put you in a room above stairs, but when I explained to Miss Meecham about the need for you to be close, it seemed to satisfy that gleam of curiosity in her beady eyes."

"Lady Southridge!" Beatrix scolded, biting back a giggle.

She paused in her relaxed amble and placed her hands on her hips as she focused on Beatrix. "Are you to say you disagree with my observation?" she dared.

Beatrix narrowed her eyes back, pausing. "No… but to say such things… why… it's simply rude."

"It's not rude if it's the truth. The woman does have beady eyes," Lady Southridge shot back. "But I see your point, which is why I will refrain from telling her."

"How noble of you," Beatrix replied cheekily.

"I rather think so."

They continued their walk and approached the orangery door. The large stone building was eggshell-white with stone corbels surrounding the upper perimeter, adding functionality and design. The windows faced south, spreading out before them as they approached the heavy wooden door. Lady Southridge twisted the handle, and it opened without so much as a creak. Immediately the scent of fertile earth and humid moisture assaulted Beatrix, comforting her, calling to her. The Orangery was easily her favorite place at Breckridge house.

They passed several stone benches facing the windows that were filtering in the light. The sound of their skirts swishing seemed overly loud in the peaceful setting, but only for a moment as Lady Southridge began speaking.

Silence wasn't her strong point.

"I love it here. So peaceful."

Beatrix bit back a laugh. How like Lady Southridge, needing to break the silence by speaking of it.

"Indeed. But I must say that my favorite part is the far corner." Beatrix nodded her head toward the back alcove.

"Mine too…" Lady Southridge agreed then turned to Beatrix, a sparkle in her green eyes. "Had I been able to have children, I dare say they would have been conceived in that very alcove."

Beatrix gasped then felt her face flame in a blush. "And to think the duke set me in your care… the scandal you speak of," she teased.

"You've known me far too long to be scandalized by anything I say." Lady Southridge waved her off. "Regardless, it *is* quite the romantic corner. Just don't let me find you using it," she warned.

"Because there are so many gentleman around here?" Beatrix glanced around the vacant orangery meaningfully.

"Not at all, but nevertheless, what type of guardian would I be if I didn't speak my piece?" She shrugged.

"No… since we have a moment, let us discuss the particulars."

"I'm quite sure I'm aware of the particulars of my situation, Lady Southridge," Beatrix replied, her tone betraying her exasperation. Hadn't they discussed this enough?

"No, I don't think I can articulate enough the need for you to be completely aware of all this entails. This is for your own protection. You're very life… we cannot afford to take it lightly.

"Very well." Beatrix sobered and turned her full

attention to Lady Southridge

The older woman gestured to a stone bench that lined the wall. "Now… because I'm in residence, there will be people who will stop by and wish to visit with me. As my companion, you'll need to make an appearance so that it will not cause some sort of mystery. Heaven only knows that mystery only makes people curious and stupid. Especially the *ton*. Therefore, you'll be introduced as my companion and then fully ignored by any that come to visit. When a lady enters the room, you'll set aside your embroidery, stand and nod, then sit and become as invisible as possible. When you are introduced, keep your head down. I'll have Mary hide as much of your glorious hair as possible." Her forehead creased as she reached out and touched Beatrix's head. "It might take some work, but I believe we can hide it under mobcap — not necessarily the fashion or even becoming for a companion — but it will be a necessary aid in this deception". She nodded. "And I do believe we'll put you in mourning colors… perhaps."

"Pardon?" Beatrix asked as she felt her jaw drop.

"Mourning colors… not the black of the first year… no, that will cause scandal… but maybe the muted colors of a widow in her second year? Yes, that will do nicely." She gave a sharp nod of approval to her own plan. "We'll also be sure you're covered up completely… maybe add a pillow here or there…" Lady Southridge tilted her head and placed her hand on her chin, evaluating.

"No. I draw the line at pillows. Next I'll be an… expectant mother as well." Beatrix shook her head.

"No, no, nothing so drastic. My dear, don't be dramatic." Lady Southridge tsked her tongue.

Beatrix narrowed her eyes. Yes… because *she* was being

the dramatic one.

"It will be like a game!" Lady Southridge exclaimed, clapping her hands and startling Beatrix.

"Yes… a game," Beatrix replied, unable to procure the same amount of enthusiasm.

"Oh posh, don't be so sour! You at least get to spend time with me," Lady Southridge remarked, grinning.

"True." And Beatrix *was* glad to spend time with her.

"Now… I suggest you enjoy your last day before we start the ruse." Lady Southridge spoke kindly as she stood and straightened her skirt. "I don't expect anyone will visit before tomorrow—"

Lady Southridge was interrupted by the sound of someone's entrance to the orangery. A maid glanced about and spotted them. With hurried steps she approached and curtsyed. "My lady, you have a caller. Trent tried to send him away, but he… well, he refused."

"Refused?"

Beatrix watched Lady Southridge's eyes widen in concern. "What exactly do you mean, Polly?" She narrowed her eyes slightly.

Polly glanced to the cobblestone floor and shifted her weight nervously. "I… that is… he was insistent and mentioned that you had left something at the Fox Inn that you'd wish returned. He refused to leave the item with Trent."

Lady Southridge sighed heavily. Turning to Beatrix, she placed her hands on her hips. "So much for our plans. Beverly? Would you please ask cook to prepare tea? We'll take it in my private chambers."

Beatrix nodded in understanding. *Beverly.* So that was going to be her name for the time being. Well, it could be worse, she decided. "Of course, my lady." Beatrix slipped into her role and curtsyed, but as she turned to leave, Lady Southridge's voice stopped her.

"Bev? Please, enjoy the orangery for just a few minutes and then be sure to slip through the servants' entrance I showed you earlier. It will take you directly to Cook." Lady Southridge's gaze was direct and shrewd, as if trying to convey additional meaning to her words.

Beatrix understood immediately. Wait first then slip inside unnoticed.

*And so it begins.*

At least she wasn't wearing the mobcap yet!

"Come, Polly. Let's go see what the ruckus is all about. I can't imagine what I left…" Lady Southridge's voice trailed off as she left with Polly.

Beatrix sighed and glanced around the vacant orangery. She walked down an aisle of potted lemon trees, reaching out and brushing leaves with her hands. Trying to ignore the cold finger of fear that tickled her heart, she tried to reason with herself. It was nigh too impossible for someone to know she had taken to hiding with Lady Southridge. It was simply a coincidence that had brought some strange gentleman to the door of Breckridge House.

When she was there…

Hiding.

Dear heavens… she needed to stop this!

Taking a deep breath, she squared her shoulders and walked over to the door. It pushed open silently and spilled in the sunshine. Her fears melting in the warmth, she walked around the back of the orangery and toward the servants' entrance.

It was a plain wooden door and opened directly into

the kitchen area of Breckridge House. Immediately the sounds of the bustling kitchen met her ears. As she rounded the stone wall, she paused at the sound of cook yelling at the scullery maid. A river of runny eggs and shattered shells dotted the wooden floor of the kitchen. A loud thud startled her as a young lad slipped on the mess, dropping his wooden bucket in the process and sending cook into another fit. Leaning back against the cool stone wall, she watched as several maids rushed forward with rags and another bucket. Beatrix paused, waiting till cook's color returned to a safer shade of pink, rather than the angry crimson that had flushed her face earlier. Clearing her throat softly, she straightened her posture away from the wall.

"Aye?" The plump woman glanced to Beatrix. Her mobcap skewed slightly with a few grey curls peeking through. Her blue eyes narrowed impatiently then softened.

"Lady Southridge requests tea served in her private chambers." Beatrix nodded slightly.

"Very well." Cook turned toward the stove, but not before glaring once again at the mess on the floor.

Sidestepping the remaining river of eggs, Beatrix made her way to the stairs that would lead to the back of the house. If she were careful, she could make it from the servants' quarters to the staircase leading to Lady Southridge's chambers without being seen.

She'd simply be cautious.

And thus was now the story of her life.

# CHAPTER TWO

Neville tapped his foot impatiently as he stared daggers at the bloody butler who had all but assaulted him with a cane.

As if sensing his thoughts, the butler jerked the cane.

Neville narrowed his eyes further, daring him to try something.

He wanted to pick a fight.

Even if it was with a bloody octogenarian butler with a wicked cane.

Footsteps in the hall pulled his attention, and he glanced from the butler to the door of the parlor where he waited.

Lady Southridge entered with a flourish of gray and emerald, an impatient expression on her face that immediately changed into one of recognition. "Lord Neville?"

"Ah, Lady Southridge." He stood and bowed, sliding his gaze to the evil butler in triumph.

"What in heaven's name are you doing here?" Lady Southridge asked.

He was about to reply when he was interrupted by a

cough from the butler.

A cough that sounded suspiciously like a laugh.

He cast a threatening glare to the old codger then turned back to Lady Southridge. "It's quite simple actually. I was staying at the same inn as you, apparently, for I came to return some misplaced items. One of which is your fine horse." He tilted his head, watching her reaction, studying it.

"Oh… well, I thank you. There was no need for you to go to such trouble," she replied coolly.

"And this." He withdrew the handkerchief and held it out for her.

"Oh… again, how kind." Her gaze narrowed.

And even a man of his merit felt the urge to squirm under her scrutiny.

"Aren't you quite the gentleman for taking such an… interest… in this?" she replied.

"It was nothing of the sort. I simply found them while searching for something else," Lord Neville replied, testing the waters.

"Were you able to find that which you were searching for?" she asked, still spearing him with her green gaze.

"Not yet. But I do believe I'm rather close."

"Indeed." Lady Southridge shrugged. "Would you care for tea?"

He tugged on his white gloves. "Tea would be delightful."

"Trent? Would you please notify cook of a change of plans? I'll take my tea here with Lord Neville."

"Of course, my lady." The butler stood, the movement punctuated by the sound his cane hitting the marbled floor with more force than necessary.

Lady Southridge glanced to him curiously at the loud thud.

"Quite the help you have here," Lord Neville spoke as the butler left.

"Loyal to a fault." She gave him a pointed glare. "Please, sit, Lord Neville." Lady Southridge invited, gesturing to a seat across from the one she had just chosen.

"Apparently," Neville spoke under his breath.

"Hmm?"

"Nothing, nothing. So, Lady Southridge, what brings you to Breckridge House? And in the middle of the Season? I do hope you are feeling well."

"Quite well. Thank you for your concern. But you see, with my brother just married to the lovely Bethanny, I do think they require some privacy. Wouldn't you agree?"

"Indeed. However, I'm afraid I'm the bearer of bad tidings then. I can only assume by your mannerisms that you have not heard." He leaned forward in his chair and folded his hands carefully. He was wary to make his expression severely concerned, even preparing to lower his tone.

"What tidings?" Lady Southridge's mannerisms were alert, disturbed.

"It would seem that one of the wards of the Duke of Clairmont, one of Bethanny's sisters, has been abducted," he whispered.

"No!" Lady Southridge immediately stood, her hand fanning herself wildly. "No, it cannot be! How was I not informed?" She walked around the chair then gripped the back carefully.

"Indeed." He nodded once.

"How is poor Bethanny doing? And Charles? Oh

heavens! I must leave for London at once! But oh! I cannot!" She placed her hand to her forehead as if about to faint.

"Are you ill?" Lord Neville stood, feeling trepidation that the woman might actually faint. Dear Lord, heaven only knew what the butler would do with the cane then!

"No… no." She took in a few steadying breaths. "I'm well. Quite… well," she answered and squared her shoulders. "You must find her!" she all but commanded.

"My lady, why do you think I'm gallivanting about the English countryside?" he asked.

"Well, how am I to know if you're on holiday or not? What *are* you doing, Lord Neville?" She placed her hands on her hips and narrowed her gaze.

"Trying to find her. And… I might add…" He took a step toward her, meeting her gaze. "…I was told something quite interesting while at the Fox Inn." He let his words linger as he watched her expression for the smallest sign of avoidance. "You see… the stable boy was quite impressed with the beauty of your traveling partner…" He took another step closer, letting the statement hang heavily in the air.

Then she laughed.

"He thought Bev was a beauty? Well, I'll have to tell her that! It should make her day, being widowed these years." She shook her head.

"Bev?" Lord Neville continued to watch her. Her laughter had taken him by surprise, but it held an edge to the sound… slightly unnatural… which kept his interest.

"Yes, Bev. My lady's companion. A very shy thing, but great for keeping an old woman like me company." She waved her hand dismissively.

"And just where did you hire Bev?" he asked, hearing skepticism lace his tone.

"In London, of course. Lady Crumpton's daughter's governess knew of a woman's son who had lost his life at sea, leaving a poor widow. Of course, she was from a prominent family but had… well, married beneath her. Ah, the things the heart does for love." She seemed to lose herself in the story as she sighed heavily and gazed into the air.

"Lady Southridge?" he called, resisting the urge to snap his fingers in front of her face. He was growing impatient.

"Oh, dear me. A thousand apologies. What was I saying?" she asked, all innocent and kind.

Neville took a calming breath. "You were telling the dramatic tale of your lady's companion," he clipped out.

"Indeed. Poor Bev… all alone, not a shilling to her name. Well, I simply *had* to take her in, you see."

"Of course." He narrowed his eyes. "Being such a close acquaintance."

"Do not mock me, young man," Lady Southridge snapped, her green eyes igniting like fire.

"I'd never dream of such a thing, my lady," he replied, bowing somberly and returning to his seat, his skin all but crawling with the suspicion that she was simply putting on a ruse.

"Of course, it's been a hard transition for her, being here… which is another reason why we left London… too many memories."

"Of her husband?" Neville asked, growing amused by her long tale in spite of himself.

"No… didn't I mention he was a sailor?" She cocked her head and pressed a finger to her chin. "Yes, I do believe

I mentioned that. Do try to keep up, Lord Neville," she scolded.

"I—"

"And do not interrupt."

He nodded, biting back a wry grin.

"Now… London was where she was raised… because, if you'll remember my story, she was from a wealthy family and simply… followed her heart."

"How tragic," he replied stoically.

"Ah! No, how *romantic.*"

"Yes, this whole story is quite the story of love." He was growing weary.

"Regardless, I shall not bore you with the details. We should not lose sight of what is important, and *that* is that you should find Beatrix." She nodded, strode to her seat, and sat with a decisive nod.

"I do believe I was trying to explain that it is, indeed, my intention to find her. Since my news came as such a shock to you, I assume you have no idea where she could have gone?" he asked.

"Hmm…" Lady Southridge's lips twisted slightly, as she appeared to think. "I do not think she'd travel to Greenford Waters on her own… and if she was taken as you say… then I'm afraid I am no help. But I must urge you onward to find her! You must not linger a single moment." She stood and waved at him to stand as well. "You must go. Now."

"Lady Southridge, I appreciate your enthusiasm, but I was going to beg a favor of you." Neville watched as she gave one final longing glace at the door then turned her eyes to him. "Would it be possible to impose on you for a few days so that I might search this area? I've visited a few inns, but I do believe I can find out more information if I'm not… shall we say… traveling as a gentleman." He lowered his chin and speared her with his gaze.

"Is that so?" Lady Southridge queried skeptically.

"Indeed. I have exhausted all other options, and I'm getting rather desperate." He took a step toward her, keeping his expression open and hopeful. What he really wanted was to be allowed access to Breckridge House… because he was quite certain that Bev, the lady's maid, was Beatrix, kidnapped ward of the duke. But what he couldn't figure out was *why* Lady Southridge had done it.

"I do believe I can help you… but I must insist that you do not stay overly long. My lady's maid… well, she gets rather shy around men, and I do not wish her to be uncomfortable."

"Thank you, Lady Southridge. Your hospitality is appreciated. I will not overstay my welcome." He bowed.

Her gaze narrowed as she studied him. Cautiously, she stood and went to ring the bell. "Trent will show you to a room."

"Delightful," he spoke then swore inwardly. Yes, that bloody butler would show him to a room with a view… off a cliff.

"If you'll excuse me then, I do believe I'll take a moment to refresh myself." She glanced to the door, and he could practically hear the churning of her mind as she bustled toward it.

"Here's your tea, my lady." Polly arrived just as Lady Southridge tried to make her escape.

"Ah, thank you. Please set it on the table there and serve Lord Neville." She turned to face him. "I'll be back down in a moment to join you."

With that, she left.

After the maid served him tea, he sipped the hot and bitter liquid, letting it warm him. There was some sort of mayhem afoot, and he was going to discover exactly what it was.

First order of business, find Bev — or Beatrix — whoever she truly was.

*The Forsaken Love of a Lord*, Book 1 of the Forsaken Lord Series. Available Now!

**THE FORSAKEN LOVE OF A LORD**

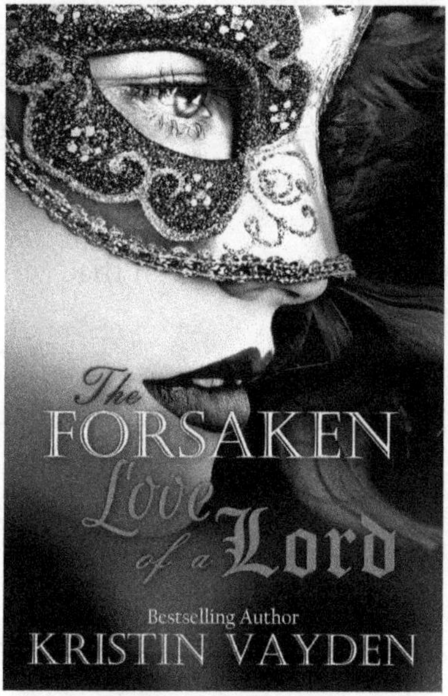


# PROLOGUE

OLIVIA PIERCE HELD her breath as she lightly tiptoed around the corner, inching closer to where her parents spoke in hushed tones. Keeping out of sight, she listened carefully to their whispered conversation, hoping for a clue.

The past few weeks since her older half-sister's death had been full of mourning and intrigue; something was afoot.

Something that *wasn't* good.

Of course, she had mourned her sister's death — as much as one could mourn a half-sister who had made her life miserable. If there was one thing for certain, in death there was peace.

A pang of guilt pinched her chest as she thought it, but it didn't hinder the truth. Peace reigned in her life now, aside from the mystery that surrounded the untimely death. It was odd. When someone died, the first question that came to mind was *How?* And with her departed sister Marybelle, that was the very question no one asked or answered.

Except for Olivia. She had asked that very question many times.

And received no answer.

Which was why she had pretended to be asleep, only to wait long enough to sneak down the stairs and, hopefully, overhear the truth. Regardless of the lack of sisterly affection she'd held, she still wanted to know what had taken Maybelle's life… and, if she were truly honest, what would happen now with Edward, Lord Langley, her late sister's husband.

She shook her head, trying to dispel the immediately vivid memories of the man who had unknowingly won her loyalty as a young child. Tall, with startlingly green eyes and an easy smile, Olivia had often wondered why someone as wonderful as Lord Langley had chosen to marry *Marybelle the Awful.*

Love had to be blind.

Her father's voice broke through her thoughts. "Regina, we have no choice. How do you not understand this? We'll be ruined! If you cannot think past yourself, at least think of Olivia. Would you take it away from her? If we leave quietly, he will not press the issue. We can return—"

"When, Preston? When can we return? When this black

stain on our good name is forgotten? You *know* the long memory of the *ton*. No matter what we do, there will be whispers. There will be talk, and it will affect her ability to make a match. If we stay and face the allegations—"

"The truth, you mean? Allegations." Her father spat the word, even in the hushed tones they used, distain dripped from every syllable. "A fine word for it. I'm sure the *ton* won't be so kind."

"How dare you! That is your daughter—"

"No, that was your daughter."

Silence.

Olivia held her breath, waiting. Never had she heard her father disown Marybelle before.

"Regardless—"

"I will not have *my* daughter's reputation smeared because of an act of folly that she had no part in, let alone understand. My word stands. We leave. He promised—"

"And you believe him? What weight does his word carry now? He is nothing to us!" Her mother shouted in a barely restrained whisper.

"He has more honor than Marybelle ever did. The fact that he's giving us a choice… when he could go to the authorities—"

"He has no proof—"

"He has his word. That's all it will take. The whisper of a scandal, and we'd be ruined. You know this."

Olivia heard her mother's deep sigh. "Then we have no choice. We'll retire to the country. We'll stay in the Sussex estate till she turns eighteen—"

"Twenty. He specifically said twenty." Her father cut in.

"Why? What does it matter if she's eighteen or twenty?"

"If my instincts are correct, he's… well, hoping that—"

"That we won't return? That we won't give her a season? What?" Her mother asked in an exasperated tone. Her irritation evident.

"He's hoping we will find her someone local, in Sussex, and he'll never have to see us. After all, a twenty year old would be in her second or even third season…"

"And on the shelf," her mother finished.

Olivia's heart soared! Was this truly the wretched issue? She had half a mind to march in there and tell them to quit their arguing over such a trivial matter! All this? Over her? She chuckled to herself. She had always loved her time in Sussex where the air was fresh; she could ride for hours — at break-neck speed — and read till dinnertime. No having to constantly change dresses, no gossiping, no foul stench or sooty skyline, just a wide horizon and a bit of refreshing rain here and there.

"If we leave, he'll keep this all to himself?" her mother asked, and Olivia leaned in to hear her father's answer, hoping he'd give more information on what exactly they were hoping to keep a secret.

"Yes. But if or when we return to London—"

"When Olivia is twenty," her mother spat.

"Indeed, then we are to not expect his attention in any way. He warned me to never address him. A cut direct would be the result."

"Which would start talk—"

"And ruin Olivia's chances."

"Miserable bast—"

"Regina!"

"Forgive me. I'm just so angry." Her mother began to cry.

"I know. I am as well. Marybelle betrayed us all. Let us

be thankful we have a chance to keep what remains of our family intact, shall we?" her father replied softly in his ever-practical manner.

"Very well. I'll instruct the servants to pack us first thing in the morning."

Olivia lightly tiptoed back to her room and slid into the blankets on her bed. Well, she had discovered part of the mystery. Half of her was relieved that they'd be leaving London; the other half was burning with curiosity. Especially since she was still unsure as to the intrigue surrounding Marybelle… and Lord Langley.

However, the joy at leaving London and the cloud of whispers behind overwhelmed the curiosity. Perhaps someday she'd know. Till then, she'd simply be thankful.

# CHAPTER ONE

## Four Years Later

EDWARD ASHLEY, THE Viscount Langley, swirled his brandy and stared into the glowing fire that was burning low in his darkened study. He knew this day would come; he'd felt it in his gut even as he had said the words four — though it felt more like forty — years earlier to his deceased wife's father.

Stepfather actually, if one was being particular.

And Edward *was* one to be particular, which was why he still called himself ten kinds of fool for falling for such a treacherous woman. How had he deluded himself to thinking he loved Marybelle? That she loved him? Ha! *That* was truly the rub. Marybelle love someone else other than herself? Impossible.

Yet, hadn't he thought that love made the impossible, possible? Yes, he had. Back when he was young, naïve, and foolish.

But no more.

No, he had learned his lesson and paid for another person's sins, over and over. Everything he had loved about Marybelle had been a lie — an elaborate game. One she had won till the night it had all come back to seek its bloody vengeance. That night, more than one kind of poetic justice had been served. It was too bad it was far too late to offer any redemption to his jaded heart.

Or perhaps it was a blessing.

If one cannot love, then one cannot hurt.

Rather they are the lifeless, a breathing shell, one he knew he had become. But the pain was less, the self-loathing diminished in the balm of time… but he'd never heal.

He didn't want to.

Notwithstanding, the Pierce family was back in London, Marybelle's young sister in tow. The once young girl was now twenty. Surely they were hoping to give her a season. He scoffed at the idea. *Marriage mart, love* — all words that held a bitter taste in his mouth like over steeped tea that had grown cold. Miserable.

He detested cold tea, part of his particular nature.

Well, he'd keep his part of the bargain as well. He'd not say a word to the *ton* about the truth of that night he'd found Marybelle.

He'd not say what had been lost.

He'd not whisper a word of what had been found.

He'd turn and walk away the moment they walked into view, because everything they represented, he wanted to forget.

And that was the very thing he was unable to ever do.

"I take it you've heard the news, then?"

Edward startled slightly at the sound of his friend's voice. With an irritated glare, he turned to watch as Curtis Sheppard entered the room.

"I take it you've forgotten how to knock again," Edward shot back.

"My, my we're surly tonight. I'll take your glower as a yes to my question." His friend strode in with easy steps, a devil-may-care-grin on his face.

Edward felt the uncharacteristic urge to beat it off him.

"You know… with all the venom coming from your expression, one might get the impression that they weren't welcome," Curtis replied offhandedly as he helped himself to a crystal glass of brandy, then sauntered over to a chair.

"Then I'd have to change my original impression," Edward replied, a slight grin bending his lips.

"Of…?" Curtis asked as he set the crystal glass of brandy down softly.

"Your intelligence. I think you're finally catching on."

"You wound me, old man. I know for a fact that I'm about the only one that bothers to stop by and at least attempt to cheer you up. Lord knows, you've scared everyone else away."

"They were quicker to get the hint."

"They were cowards," Curtis shot back, his eyebrows raised, daring him to refute his claim.

Edward glanced down at the Aubusson carpet, studying it but not seeing it.

Damn the man, he had a point. But Curtis always did. He was one of the only friends that continued to endure Edward's surly nature. Always cheerful, it was annoying as hell, but he broke up the monotony. He was one of the only people in the world who knew the truth, and Edward trusted him to keep it. That type of loyalty was rare as hen's teeth. For that, Curtis had his loyalty as well, though Edward had, through the years, forgotten how to display any other emotion other than anger… or remorse.

Edward's gaze lifted as he watched Curtis approach

him. "Yes?"

Curtis' eyes were narrowed slightly, and he took a position just to the side of Edward and began to study the ground. "Just wondering what you found so damn interesting about the carpet that's been in this study since you were in short pants."

Edward shoved his friend good-naturedly, a grin breaking through.

"And here I had thought you'd lost the ability to smile. My hope in your black soul is restored." Curtis shrugged and sipped his brandy.

"I'd not place so much faith in me."

"I'll be sure to underestimate," Curtis shot back and returned to his chair. "So, back to my original reason for gracing you with my company—"

"I'd rather not talk about it," Edward cut in, spearing his friend with a glare.

"I'm sure you'd rather rot. However, that doesn't change the fact that you'll be seeing them at some point or another. What is your plan? After all, you're Edward Ashley, Viscount Langley." He raised his eyebrows. "You plan your life down to what you'll dream about."

"Revenge."

"Bloody business. Best served cold, eh? You're above that. I'll not let you delude yourself."

"What—"

"I know enough. Leave it. It will only blacken your heart more. Besides, if you ruin the family, you'll be going back on *your* word… which we both know will not happen. As much of an old stick you've become, you're not dishonorable."

"Blast you, Curtis."

"Thank you. I'll take that as a compliment, simply assuring myself that you see my brilliant point."

"You are vexing beyond words," Edward muttered.

"I've been told I'm many things beyond words… however, most of those comments are from the lady population." He grinned.

"Only you could find some way to make me actually *want* to discuss your sordid love life in efforts to escape the previous topic of conversation. How do you do it?" Edward asked in a wry tone.

"I'm far more brilliant than you give me credit for. It's the looks. Most people take one look at me and think, *'Ah! All beauty, no brains.'* For honestly, it isn't fair that I have a lion's share of both." Curtis sighed as if pained by it.

"And humility, scads of that as well." Edward shook his head.

"I'm quite proud of that particular virtue, yes." Curtis laughed. "Now, I'm going to attend the Bridgeton rout tomorrow. A certain someone will be there. Alaina…" He let the name linger.

Edward glanced heavenward, praying for deliverance to a God he wasn't sure cared about him anymore.

At one time he had been so sure.

Now he was quite the opposite.

"Alaina?" Edward repeated.

"Yes, goddess of beauty herself."

"And voice of a minion."

"Do not say such things! Her voice is delightful… unique," he added with a flourish of his hand.

"Annoying, not unique… annoying. I swear, I would rather listen to the screeching of fighting tomcats rather than hear her speak in that high-pitched, nasal tone."

"You hide your true opinions so well," Curtis replied dryly.

Edward scowled.

"At least I know I'll have no competition from you. She'll be mine for the taking." He rubbed his hands together.

"I'd not dare stand in the way of true love," Edward mocked.

Curtis shook his head and chuckled. "At least love for the moment."

"One day, you'll find some lady that will turn your head in such a way you'll not even be enticed by another… and I predict that very lady will not give you the time of day. God's way of punishing you for your many sins." Edward spoke clearly as he strode to the wide chair behind his desk.

"Love advice? From you? My, it is a night of miracles," Curtis replied with a mocking grin.

"Insolent—"

"Don't be irritated at my keen observation and ability to articulate it so clearly. Now, back to the Bridgeton rout. You'll attend, of course." Curtis brushed some lint from his fine coat.

"No."

"Yes."

"I'll not repeat myself."

"Yes, you'll attend! You gave your word two weeks ago. I knew you'd try to back out of our agreement since the arrival of Pierce family, but I shall not let you. I've been working on sweet Alaina for some time now. This is my chance." He smacked his knee and stood. "You know I need you to attend if I'm to be allowed entrance."

"Bloody hell, why in the world do you wish to be part

of the *ton*? Have you met any of them? Vipers, the lot of them."

"I've met you," Curtis shot back.

Edward rolled his eyes in exasperation.

"You attended the Blackwood party without me—"

"But that was far less exclusive than the Bridgeton event. You know this." Curtis all but whined.

Edward frowned.

He hated that his friend had a point. While Curtis was wealthier than Croesus, his money was made in trade, not inherited from an age-old title.

And his father, being the independent type, had refused to try and purchase a title on the sly, so their family was, while wealthy, still part of the blue-collar variety. And being part of that class eliminated them from receiving invitations from the exclusive parties of the *ton*.

Lucky blackguard.

So unless Edward brought him along, he'd not be able to attend. And as much as he wished it weren't true, he *had* said he'd attend.

"I loathe you," Edward ground out in defeat.

"It's perfectly alright. I *adore* you enough for the both of us." Curtis fanned himself like a lady.

Edward snorted.

Curtis grinned. "The lengths you push me to in order to lift your spirits. I'd think you be wise to thank the good Lord for such a friend as I." Curtis nodded. Taking a moment to drain his brandy, he released a satisfied sigh and stood. "I'll see you on the morrow. And… do try to smile. We wouldn't want to frighten anyone," he replied with an easy smirk and left.

Edward shook his head and stood to go and study the

fire once more.

But even for the warm heat from the fire's soft glow, his heart chilled, knowing that tomorrow, he'd have to face the very people he never want to see again.

Damn it all.

# CHAPTER TWO

Olivia blinked as she studied herself in the vanity mirror. Her shoulders rose and fell with each breath she took, yet the rhythmic cadence didn't settle her swirling emotions, her anxiety.

Why, oh *why* had they needed to come back to London? It had been so perfectly pleasant in Sussex with the wild wood behind the manor and the freedom to ride each day. It had been a dream.

And like a dream, had a distinct end.

She felt as if she were awakening from a cocoon of peace and thrown into a typhoon of activity and expectations — none of which she accomplished with grace. They had arrived a full week ago, and in that time her mother had packed their lives with more activity than the four previous years combined.

The modiste, the haberdasher, the modiste again, tea with old friends, those same old friends visiting and gossiping.

Oh, dear Lord, the gossip.

If she heard any more about Lady Woolworth's out-of-fashion wig, or last season's blue that was foolishly worn by some unfortunate spinster, she would scream.

*Loudly.*

Why were people so petty? Why did they even *care?* If those old clucking hens had nothing else to do other than chip away at others, then their opinions shouldn't matter.

It wasn't as if they were doing anything of value with *their* lives.

She'd mentioned as much to her mother.

Her mother had paused midstride. A second later, she spun then speared her with an icy glare. "You'll never say such things out loud, again. *Understood*? You have a reputation to create. You have your name, your father's title, the rest is up to you and you *will* make us proud." She'd taken a step toward Olivia, her cold gaze narrowing. "Have I made myself utterly clear?" She'd articulated with lethal grace.

Olivia couldn't find her voice. Never before had she seen such ice in her mother's tone.

Unless someone mentioned Marybelle's name.

Or Lord Langley's.

But that was beside the point.

In that moment, her mother had been a stranger; rather, she'd looked just like those old biddies that Olivia had been speaking of.

It had been a chilling awakening; one she hadn't quite recovered from. And she was beginning to realize that this whole return to London had one goal: she was a lamb to the slaughter. Already her mother had given her a *list,* of all things, naming the appropriate gentlemen for her to marry.

Marry, and she hadn't been to one ball yet.

Wasn't that all a bit premature?

It wasn't as if she *had* to marry immediately. Why was

her mother pushing her?

She dared not ask, not after the ice that chilled her from the first question. Though she hadn't ever been particularly close to her mother, the separation in their relationship only seemed to grow as time went on… especially now.

A calculating glint in her mother's eye caused a chill to prickle Olivia's flesh whenever they were in company. And for that reason she had avoided her mother as much as possible.

"Are you ready, Olivia?" her mother's refined voice asked coolly as she began to twist the knob leading to the bedroom.

"Yes," Olivia answered, because it was pointless to be anything but honest.

Her mother strode into the room, her eyes immediately assessing Olivia. "Oh, my! You're breathtaking! Surely all the gentlemen will flock to your side in efforts to secure a dance!" She clapped her hands. "Hmm." She paused and walked around Olivia, studying her closely. Her eyes narrowed slightly, causing a *V* to form in her forehead. Tugging at the fabric on her bodice, she shifted the neckline of the dress slightly, lowering it.

Olivia was quite sure it had already been too low.

"That's better. We need you to draw everyone's eye."

Apparently those eyes weren't to be focused on her face.

"Now, chin up, give a dazzling smile to each person who approaches you, and remember, under no circumstances—"

"Am I to speak to Lord Langley," Olivia finished, though her tone was more exasperated than anything else.

"Yes. Now, I'll wait for you downstairs. Your father has already ordered the carriage to be brought around front.

Don't dally." Her mother nodded once and left in a flurry of emerald-green silk.

Olivia sighed in relief when her mother's form disappeared from the room. Taking a deep breath, she glanced once again to the mirror. Would people compare her to her sister Marybelle? She hoped not. Although, it helped that she looked quite different. Everything about Marybelle was rich, from the color of her lush crown of sable hair to her dark cinnamon eyes. Olivia took after her father's side. Her slightly wavy hair was the color of butter — or so her mother had once said — and her eyes were a light blue. Where Marybelle had been soft and rounded, Olivia was more petite in stature and in form.

Olivia turned and evaluated herself once more, it was going to be such a bother tonight, to smile and play the pretty and ignorant debutant, especially when all she wanted to do was leave the sure-to-be-stuffy ballroom.

But there was one secret hope she harbored. Though she knew she was forbidden to speak with Lord Langley, there was no rule about *looking* at him. How she hoped he'd attend tonight. It was the one bright spot in the evening. Would he look the same? Would he remember her? Would his memories be of the innocent and playful variety before everything happened with Marybelle? Or would he look at her and simply see her sister and all the pain she had caused? It seemed as if the man he had *become* overshadowed the man he *was*, the man she remembered. Others saw his hardened heart, the reclusive exterior, but Olivia remembered the man she knew hid within.

While the rumor — which she'd learned from the aforementioned old clucking hens — was that he was after revenge. Olivia had made the decision to pursue something far more dangerous.

His heart.

"Olivia!" her mother's voice called.

"I'm on my way," Olivia called back and strode to the door. Pausing, she grasped the top of her dress and pulled it up, higher than it was before her mother had *adjusted* it. "Much better," she mumbled and left.

"HERE WE ARE." Curtis rubbed his gloved hands together, the stark white of their soft leather in bright contrast with his evening kit.

"Indeed. Please allow a moment for my heart to recover from its delighted racing," Edward replied with more than a hint of sarcasm.

Curtis ignored him; already his eyes were scanning the sea of men and women, searching for Alaina.

"Why her? I've never understood… I'm assuming it's a passing fancy," Edward asked quietly.

"Of course it's a passing fancy! She's a widow, she's wealthy, and she has no need for any strings to support her…" Curtis wagged his eyebrows.

"Rake."

"Why, thank you."

"I wasn't saying it as a compliment."

"Oh, I'll still pretend you did." He shrugged and returned to his search.

"Delude yourself all you wish," Edward mumbled back.

Curtis gasped and smacked Edward's chest. "Please tell

me that angel that just walked in with Lord Pierce is *not* Marybelle's sister. Lie, if you must."

Edward was watching Curtis' expression.

*Bloody hell.*

Curtis had the far-off, lovesick-swain appearance of one besotted.

He didn't want to look. He didn't want to think. All he wanted to do was turn around and walk back out the door and drink himself stupid at White's.

Because he was quite sure it *was* her.

But he was curious… damn it all. So with a fortifying breath, he followed Curtis' fixed gaze.

It sure as hell was Olivia, Marybelle's young half-sister. As a child, she had been adorable, sweet, and kind — truthfully, everything that Marybelle hadn't been. Though in his defense, he hadn't known it. Olivia had grown from that adorable little girl to a diamond of the first water. Her golden hair glittered like a halo as she walked gracefully into the room. The soft lavender pigment of her dress somehow highlighted the creamy hue of her skin. He couldn't see her eyes from this distance, but he was sure they'd be a sparkling blue, just as he remembered them. Her body was petite, yet perfectly proportioned; her gown accentuated the fact far too clearly. Edward cleared his throat and glanced away. His eyes scanned the room, searching for distraction. "I think I see Alaina," he remarked in a tight tone.

"Alaina who?" Curtis replied breathlessly. "I need an introduction — damn it all. You can't do that. Hmm." His gaze darted about the room.

"Nice to know I have your unyielding loyalty," Edward remarked.

"You know you do! I've been here from the beginning… but just because her sister was Delilah — from the Bible. You know, Samson and Delilah?"

"I bloody hell well know what you're talking about, Curtis," Edward ground out.

"Splendid. Just making sure. But what I was saying—"

"Yes, I get it, just because her sister was a miserable excuse for a human being, doesn't mean that she will be."

"Exactly."

"But I'm not going to find out," Edward asserted.

Curtis paused, watching him. His gaze shifted to Olivia then back to Edward. "Fine, but I sure as hell am."

"You are certainly free to do as you wish, but you will *not* involve me in any way. Understood?" Edward turned to face his friend. Waiting for a response, he held his gaze.

"Very well." Curtis bowed and sauntered way, circling the ballroom, though Edward noticed his gaze continued to stray to where Olivia was practically holding court with several anxious young bucks all vying for her attention. Anger swirled in his chest, constricting his lungs and stealing his breath.

It was too alike, too close. Hadn't it been the same with Marybelle? Wasn't *he* one of the lovesick swains who had surrounded her like a bee to honey?

And he'd been stung.

Over and over, till he didn't feel the pain any longer.

Till the pain became his normal; till the day the stinging stopped, and he was too overjoyed to mourn his own wife's demise.

Curtis had manipulated some poor chap into giving him an introduction to Miss Olivia. He bowed sharply; Olivia curtsyed and extended her slender hand for him to take. From here, Edward could see her enchanting grin, far different than her sister's.

Which was a blessing.

He didn't think he could stomach any other similarities.

Curtis tipped his head and gestured to the dance floor, and she nodded, following him on the floor as the music shifted to a waltz.

Unable to stand it any longer, Edward turned and headed to the door, only nodding twice to a few gentlemen who were arriving late. Once out the door and in his carriage, he demanded his coachmen take him to White's. Halfway there, he changed his mind and headed home instead.

Drinking only made the memories sharper.

And, more than anything, tonight he wanted everything completely dull.

HE IS HERE! Olivia thought excitedly as she tried to keep her gaze from continuously straying to his person. He was even more handsome than she remembered. His coal-colored hair was swept back immaculately, accenting the light blue of his eyes—that she couldn't quite see but most assuredly remembered—and the olive tone of his skin. Her heart thumped in her chest at the sight of him. How she wished there was some way to at least approach him, but it was impossible.

Drat.

Her attention strayed to the gentleman beside him.

They seemed to be in easy conversation. Was he perhaps a friend?

*Interesting.*

A friend wouldn't be off limits to converse with. Now, if only she could somehow secure an introduction.

As if hearing her thoughts, Lord Langley's gaze shifted toward her. Quickly she glanced away and tried to focus on one of the gentleman who had come near to secure an introduction.

After curtsying and promising him a dance later, she risked a glance back toward Lord Langley.

But no sooner had she focused on his person did she notice that the friend was making his way toward her, as if in efforts to secure an introduction as well.

What luck!

Olivia met his gaze and gave him what she hoped was a welcoming smile. He was in the company of one of her mother's friends, no doubt with the intention of presenting him.

"Ah, Miss Olivia, may I introduce Mr. Sheppard? He's a long acquaintance of our family." Lady Maxwell simpered, her eyes dancing as she ran her gaze up Mr. Sheppard's body.

Olivia resisted the urge to shudder.

"A delight, Miss Olivia." The gentleman bowed.

"A pleasure, Mr. Sheppard."

"A beautiful lady such as yourself should not be forced to endure so many introductions without a chance to escape to the dance floor. May I have the honor of the next set?" he asked, his tone light and his eyes twinkling.

"Of course," Olivia replied immediately, not willing to risk missing out on what could be her only chance to uncover some of the mystery behind Lord Langley.

And as luck would have it, the first strains of a waltz began just as he extended his hand.

"So, Miss Olivia, tell me, why I haven't had the pleasure of dancing with you before?" Mr. Sheppard asked smoothly.

Olivia was quite sure he was a charmer, a rogue of the finest variety, but also utterly harmless. His eyes were too joyful, too full of fun. If he were a serious rake, he'd be far more… direct.

Or so she assumed.

"Well, Mr. Sheppard, we only just arrived in London this week," she answered.

"Then I'm most fortunate to have found you so near to your arrival." He winked in a playful manner, his caramel-colored eyes dancing with amusement. His light brown hair hung in carefree waves that brushed his forehead. He was broad-shouldered, the fact accentuated by the nip and tuck of his evening kit.

"Ah, what a flatterer, but I suppose it's all part of the game." She shrugged lightly.

"Game?" he asked as his eyebrows rose.

"Yes. I must admit that I'm quite frank, Mr. Sheppard. Which brings me to my point."

"Point?" He blinked, as if uncertain to be dubious or impressed.

"Yes. Now, I noticed that you were speaking with a particular gentleman earlier," Olivia hedged, her heartbeat increasing in cadence as she said the words. Immediately, a vision of Edward, Lord Langley, flashed in her mind's eye. His jet-black hair and olive-colored skin were unmistakable; however, what she had found most changed was his expression. Even from a distance, she could easily decipher a frown as he glanced in her direction. Her study of him had been quick, hopefully unnoticed. But necessary.

"I talked with quite a few gentlemen tonight, Lady Olivia," Mr. Sheppard replied carefully.

"Unless I'm underestimating your intelligence, which I highly doubt, I'm quite certain you're aware of which gentleman I'm referring to."

"My, you *are* frank."

"It's a curse, or so my mother says. I'd rather think of it as a blessing myself," she added, a slight teasing grin tipping her lips.

"You know…" Mr. Sheppard leaned forward slightly. "…I rather agree with you."

"Thank you." She felt a blush accent her cheeks.

"To answer your question, I was speaking with Lord Langley. I arrived with him actually." Mr. Sheppard was watching her closely; his smiling eyes now clear with a keen intelligence.

"Oh?" Olivia replied, struggling to keep her raging curiosity in check.

"Yes, and I must say, Miss Olivia, as much as your curiosity is surprising, it is also unwise. Lord Langley is not one you should be concerned about. Any suspicions, any… curiosities…" He paused, his gaze piercing and undeviating, as if trying to communicate something unspoken. "…are best left unexplored."

The music stopped and he bowed. When he rose, his face held a polite grin, though his gaze was still startlingly direct.

"I bid you goodnight, Miss Olivia." And he turned and left.

Olivia watched as he wove around the people and made

his way to the exit. He didn't pause or search for another partner for the upcoming quadrille; rather, he disappeared into the night.

*Odd.*

But before Olivia could think further on the subject, her next dance partner approached.

Later.

After all, she was in London… and while her mother might have different plans for her, Olivia knew her course… and all she had was time.

# About The Author

KRISTIN's inspiration for the romance she writes comes from her tall, dark and handsome husband with killer blue eyes. With five children to chase, she is never at a loss for someone to kiss, something to cook or some mess to clean but she loves every moment of it! Life is full—of blessings and adventure! Needless to say she's a big fan of coffee and wine…and living in Washington she's within walking distance of both! Follow her on Facebook (www.facebook.com/kristinvaydenauthor) And Instagram @kristinkatjoyce and Twitter @KristinVayden! You can also sign up for her newsletter at http://eepurl.com/795f9.

Acknowledgments

THANK YOU TO Blue Tulip Publishing for all the love and support they pour into every manuscript. Thank you also to my family who puts up with unfolded laundry and a distracted mom. But above all, thank you Jesus for the blessing of doing something I absolutely love, and the blessing of meeting readers, who become friends, who in turn bless me each day.

# Also From Blue Tulip Publishing

BY MEGAN BAILEY
*There Are No Vampires in this Book*

BY ELISE FABER
*Phoenix Rising*
*Dark Phoenix*
*Phoenix Freed*
*From Ashes*
*Blocked*

BY STEPHANIE FOURNET
*Butterfly Ginger*
*Leave A Mark*
*You First*

BY MARK FREDERICKSON & MELORA PINEDA
*The Emerald Key*

BY JENNIFER RAE GRAVELY
*Drown*
*Rivers*

BY LESLIE HACHTEL
*The Dream Dancer*

BY E.L. IRWIN
*Out of the Blue*
*The Lost and Found*

BY J.F. JENKINS
*The Dark Hour*

BY AM JOHNSON
*Still Life*
*Still Water*
*Still Surviving*
*Now & Forever Still*

BY A.M. KURYLAK
*Just a Bump*

BY KRISTEN LUCIANI
*Nothing Ventured*
*Venture Forward*

BY KELLY MARTIN
*Betraying Ever After*
*The Beast of Ravenston*
*The Glass Coffin*

BY NADINE MILLARD
*An Unlikely Duchess*
*Seeking Scandal*
*The Mysterious Miss Channing*
*Highway Revenge*
*The Spy's Revenge*
*The Captain's Revenge*
*The Hidden Prince*

BY BRITTNEY MULLINER
*Begin Again*

BY MYA O'MALLEY
*Wasted Time*
*A Tale as Old as Time*

BY LINDA OAKS

*Chasing Rainbows*

*Finding Forever*

*The Way Home*

*Fighting For A Chance*

BY C.C. RAVANERA

*Dreamweavers*

BY KV RIDER

*The Real Winner*

BY GINA SEVANI

*Beautifully Damaged*

*Beautifully Devoted*

BY ANGELA SCHROEDER

*The Second Life of Magnolia Mae*

*Jade*

BY T.C. SLONAKER

*The Amity of the Angelmen*

BY K.S. SMITH & MEGAN C. SMITH

*Hourglass*

*Hourglass Squared*

*Hourglass Cubed*

BY MEGAN C. SMITH

*Expired Regrets*

*Secret Regrets*

BY CARRIE THOMAS

*Hooked*

BY LORI THOMAS HARRINGTON

*The Point*

BY NICOLE THORN

*What Lies Beneath*

*Your Heart Is Mine*

BY RACHEL VAN DYKEN

*Upon a Midnight Dream*

*Whispered Music*

*The Wolf's Pursuit*

*When Ash Falls*

*The Ugly Duckling Debutante*

*The Seduction of Sebastian St. James*

*An Unlikely Alliance*

*The Redemption of Lord Rawlings*

*The Devil Duke Takes a Bride*

*Savage Winter*

*Every Girl Does It*

*Divine Uprising*

BY KRISTIN VAYDEN

*To Refuse a Rake*

*Surviving Scotland*

*Living London*

*Redeeming the Deception of Grace*

*Knight of the Highlander*

*The Only Reason for the London Season*

*What the Duke Wants*

*To Tempt an Earl*

*The Forsaken Love of a Lord*

*A Tempting Ruin*

*A Night Like No Other*

*The One*

*How to Silence a Rogue*

BY JOE WALKER
*Blood Bonds*

BY KELLIE WALLACE
*Her Sweetest Downfall*

BY C. MERCEDES WILSON
*Hawthorne Cole*
*Secret Dreams*

BY GRACIE WILSON
*Beautifully Destroyed*

BY K.D. WOOD
*Unwilling*
*Unloved*

BOX SET — MULTIPLE AUTHORS
*Forbidden*
*Hurt*
*Frost: A Rendezvous Collection*
*A Christmas Seduction*
*Christmas at Brentwood Abbey*

BLUE TULIP
PUBLISHING

www.bluetulippublishing.com

CPSIA information can be obtained
at www.ICGtesting.com
Printed in the USA
LVHW011450030222
709989LV00007B/640

9 781543 295092